BONE DANCER

SHALL WE DANCE?

ANNA-MARIE MORGAN

Copyright © 2018 by Anna-marie Morgan

All rights reserved.

No part of this book may be reproduced in any form or by any electronic or mechanical means, including information storage and retrieval systems, without written permission from the author, except for the use of brief quotations in a book review.

Cover by SelfPubBookCovers/mmrainey

For my family, with love

1
WHITE LADY

The car rounded the corner at speed. Thumping over cat's eyes. Swerving hard, to avoid the hedge. The driver squinted, his double vision the result of too many pints at the local.

As a light mist swirled in the headlights, the ambient temperature dropped. The White Lady. A shiver ran the length of his spine.

A van materialised in the gloom. Centre of the Road. Slamming his foot on the brake, he swung to the left.

In a hail of screeching and debris, he ploughed into the undergrowth. "Learn to drive you..."

The offender had gone.

Wheels spun as he threw the gearstick into reverse and hammered on the accelerator. He was going nowhere. The engine, eaten by foliage. Windscreen wipers bashed the branches in vain.

"Damned idiot!" Turning off the ignition, he pushed the door open with a tremulous hand and stumbled onto the tarmac, feeling inside his jacket pocket for his mobile.

After several goes at punching in the correct number, he slurred into the handset. "Deb?"

"Mike, where are you? It's way past midnight."

"Had a few with the lads." He staggered to where his bonnet had been swallowed by greenery. "I need you. I've had an accident."

He told her where he was, apologising umpteen times, before ambling further along the lane. He decided it best, given his current condition, to report the incident the following day. Sober. Loss of licence meant loss of livelihood. He couldn't risk that.

He wandered until he found metal gates, at the entrance to a field. Sat against them, he phoned his wife again.

"I'm by a... a... Agh! Agh!"

"What? What is it? Mike?"

∼

Yvonne rubbed her eyes, blinking at the clock. Just gone one. She had slept for only an hour and forty-nine minutes. Murder was no respecter of downtime.

She swung her legs out of bed, keeping the phone to her ear. "Where?"

"Just outside Abermule." The DCI yawned.

"I'll be there."

"Emergency vehicles are en route and should arrive any minute. I will join you as soon as I can."

"Right. See you then." She made a mental list of requirements, padding across the wooden floorboards to grab clothes. Nerve-tingling goosebumps prickled her skin.

∼

Half an hour later, she arrived at the myriad lights, bouncing around the hedgerows, surrounded by ambulances, police cars and tape. She left her Renault in a lay-by, out of the way, and approached the outer cordon.

Two paramedics in yellow and green jumpsuits passed by, shoulders hunched.

The male shook his head. "Someone's idea of a joke."

"Sorry?" Yvonne frowned.

"It's a prop from a medical school. A skeleton, threaded together and dressed in rags."

"Oh." She suppressed a smile.

His female colleague tutted as they headed to their ambulance.

The DI pursed her lips and approached the plastic suits, talking amongst themselves. She recognised pathologist Roger Hanson. He was scratching his beard, his brow furrowed.

Someone grabbed her arm.

She swung into the DCI's chest. "Chris." Her heart thumped, her mind on edge.

"Yvonne."

She cleared her throat. "Could be a prank..."

"So I'm told." He nodded towards a disappearing ambulance and rubbed his eyes. "You should get back to bed. I'll wait until the pathologist confirms it's all a joke. They booked the bloke who phoned it in. His truck is in the hedge. Drunk as a lord. Station bed-and-breakfast for him."

∼

"I'll stay, if that's okay." She pointed to where the pathologist kneeled, torch in mouth, gloved hands examining something in front of him. "He's not done, yet."

She understood why the witness had called them. The effigy sat against the field gate, knees raised. Matted hair placed on the skull. The jaw hung open as though screaming. Clothed in a ragged top and dark skirt, it was a macabre sight. A handbag dangled from the left shoulder, the arm draped over it.

"Body's been there for a while," she quoted, looking sideways at Llewellyn and grinning.

"Hilarious." He grimaced. "Such a waste of resources. We don't even have an arrestable offence."

"There's no law against dressing up scientific exhibits and leaving them to scare your friends."

"In the small hours, there should be." Llewellyn groaned. "This better not be a *thing*."

"What do you mean?"

"Remember last year? The best dressed scarecrow competition?"

"Ah, yes, I remember. Gave several people frights in the night."

Roger shouted to his team. "Bring the boards out." To the approaching officers, he barked, "You'll need scrubs."

The DI's face sobered. "What have you found?"

"Somebody cleaned the bones. But, they've been in the soil. Look..." He held up the figure's torn blouse, shining his torch into the rib cage. "One of the spinal vertebrae had a crossbow missile attached to it using one millimetre gauge wire, the same used to articulate the skeleton."

The detectives finished suiting up and knelt on the metal risers, peering into the cavity.

"Damage to ribs and spine are consistent with being shot with that bolt. We must treat this as a murder scene. We'll get everything photographed and back to the lab. I suspect the victim is female."

The DI closed her mouth. A pale mist swirled at her feet. She placed her shaking hands deep in her pockets.

2

FOREVER GRAVE

A week later, the autopsy was complete. The pathologist agreed to brief Yvonne and Dewi prior to releasing his report, as yet unfinished.

"You've got two of us, today." Roger Hanson held an arm towards his companion, a man ten years his junior. "This is Wyn Sealander, a forensic anthropologist. Teaches in Dundee. He's helping us make sense of the remains."

Yvonne offered a latex-covered hand.

Sealander took it, flicking mousey-blonde hair from his eyes.

The DI estimated him to be six foot tall, handsome and early-to-mid thirties. She smiled. "Pleased to meet you, Mr Sealander. That's an unusual name, are your family from Germany?"

"Yes." He smiled. "My father moved here from Bremen."

"You live in Dundee?"

"I flit between Dundee and here." Wyn rubbed his chin with the back of his glove. "I have a bachelor pad in Powys." His gaze met hers. Its intensity surprised her. She got a good glimpse of those vivid-blue irises, rimmed with dark grey. Long eyelashes lent him a sensitive air. He was striking.

Their attention returned to the trolley and Yvonne examined the remains, imagining the girl's face, long and narrow, with a rounded jaw.

As though reading her thoughts, Wyn touched the skull's forehead. "I'll be completing the facial reconstruction to help you identify her."

Hanson waved a gloved hand. "She was tall. Five-foot-nine." He cleared his throat. "It's difficult to say exactly when she died. If we get a name, we'll know the date she was last seen, which will help narrow the timeframe. Her age was between eighteen and twenty-two years and she had never given birth. A shot to the heart is what killed her. The angle of penetration, suggests the missile tore her aorta."

"She bled to death?" Yvonne asked, her eyes still on the bones.

"Yes, she most likely died from internal bleeding and resultant cardiac failure. We extracted DNA from the bones and compared it to samples from the red hair. Enough alleles matched to be conclusive. In other words, the hair left on top of the skull was hers."

"What about dental records?" Yvonne asked.

"We've searched extensively, but haven't found a match. Sorry. That's where Wyn comes in, with his facial reconstruction. We're following up with spectroscopy on the bone mineral content, to know where she came from. It's possible she's a foreign national."

Dewi was making notes of his own. "Let me get this straight, the killer buried her and then exhumed the body ages afterwards?"

"That's the way it reads." Hanson pointed to the broken

vertebra which had stopped the bolt from exiting the victim's back. "The perp boiled the bones, getting rid of the remaining flesh. But the porous bone, and inside the vertebrae, show traces of dirt and mineral deposits which resisted cleaning."

Yvonne leaned closer. "So, he kills her, buries her and then goes to the trouble to dig her up, wash her, and put her on display. He connects the bones with wire using a fine drill bit, and helps us by showing how he dispatched her."

"That's how it looks. I wonder what a clinical psychologist would make of that?"

She thought of Tasha. "Fascinating... Do you think the clothes were hers?"

"We believe so. The perpetrator washed them, but they had rotted in the soil, along with the body."

"Wow." She pursed her lips. "This is a whole different ball game."

"Sure is." Hanson reached behind him, pulling out a roll of metal wire. "Supplied by most DIY shops and ironmongers. I've sent samples to specialist labs for testing, to see if we can get a batch number and date."

"That's good work. Thank you, Roger."

"No problem, Yvonne. You just have to name the lass and find her murderer."

"Sounds easy." Yvonne's gaze moved to the window. "It never is."

∼

DEWI SPRINTED down the corridor towards her.

Yvonne held out a hand. "Hey, what's the hurry?"

He paused to catch breath. "Just had West Mercia on the phone. They think they've found the grave, ma'am."

"Grave?"

"That's right, ma'am. They think it belongs to our mystery woman. It contained scraps of clothing which appear to match the rags we found on her. Samples are with the lab for confirmation. Early microscopy suggests the fibres are the same."

"Where is it?"

"Long Mynd. It's parkland, owned by the National Trust. A designated area of natural beauty, in the Shropshire Hills. Someone dug up her up and left the hole open for park staff or the public to find. There's a mound of excavated soil next to the opening."

"Wow. I'm impressed they linked it to our victim so fast."

"The power of databases." He smiled.

"Are they still working up there?"

"Yes, they are."

"Mm. So, our perp not only displayed the body, he also exposed where he buried her.

"Yeah."

"What killer does that?"

"Ours, apparently."

"Okay. Let's find out what we've got."

∽

WIND RACED ACROSS THE MOOR, stinging her face like a slap. Yvonne repositioned her scarf to better protect her neck, imagining a young woman frightened and alone. Alone, except for her killer.

The scenery was stark in places. Stretched between Bishop's Castle, Church Stretton and across the rocky Stiperstones. The land appeared scarred and scraped. Hills and mountains pierced the sky. A ruggedness, which challenged you to conquer it. The killer knew this place well. She shuddered, as the hackles rose on her neck.

Reading her thoughts, Dewi completed a three-hundred-and-sixty degree turn, as though memorising every crag. "Do you think he killed her here? Brought her for a picnic, intending to take her life?"

Yvonne pursed her lips. "Down there," she pointed towards Carding Mill valley, a popular tourist site, "I'd have said no way. Too many people. But up here? Yes."

They walked the winding track to where police tape circled the burial site. Two SOCO personnel chatted near parked vehicles.

"They're busy," The DI frowned, as she and her DS continued up the path.

A guy in a shirt, tie, and a long mac came towards them. "Are you the officers from Dyfed-Powys?" He slowed and placed his hands in his trouser pockets. His eyes were as dark as his mid-length hair.

She smiled. "We are. I'm Yvonne Giles and this is Dewi Hughes."

"Nice to meet you." He nodded. "DS Will Tozer. I believe we've got missing pieces to your puzzle."

"You have. Can we see?"

"Sure. Follow me." He left the way he had come.

The DI jogged, to keep up, glad of her sensible shoes.

Several crows descended, attracted by the activity and smell. Yvonne stared into the neat hole. "Did he leave a marker?"

"A grave stone, you mean?" DS Tozer scratched his cheek, stooping to sit on his heels.

"Yes, so he would remember where he buried her."

"Not that we found. But, look around you. The views.

The Stiperstones. It wouldn't be hard to find this spot again. He might have taken photographs or made drawings."

"I'll go explore." Dewi set off towards the parked cars.

Yvonne approached the hole, resting on her heels next to Tozer. "Was anything else in the grave, besides tattered clothing?"

"No. Whoever took the body, left just enough material for us to match it to your victim. We've confirmed that a body was here, and that it decayed here. We haven't been able to match DNA. The stuff we isolated was too degraded."

"The clothing should be enough confirmation. But, I don't get it." Yvonne turned. "I mean, look at this place. This is a forever grave. Somewhere you'd bury someone if you didn't want them found. Why dig them up and display them at all? You commit the perfect murder, then years later broadcast it to the world."

"Seems like we're dealing with a narcissist. He made her hard to find, and we didn't find her. So now he's given us a little help."

Yvonne shook her head. "I don't know... I wonder if he killed her up here?"

"Unless we find a matching crossbow bolt, we may never know."

"Did you find footprints?" She levelled her gaze at him.

"SOCO made found a few. Can't guarantee they are from our guy, though. Ramblers come through here on a semi-regular basis. The numbers will increase as we head towards summer. But we'll give you what we develop and you can compare them to any you found near your deposition site."

"That would be helpful." She rubbed her chin. "What if it wasn't the killer?"

"Sorry?"

"What if someone else wanted to expose the crime?"

"Well, you said yourself, this is a place you could bury someone without anyone ever discovering them. If someone other than the killer exhumed her, they must have known she'd been murdered and who the perpetrator was. Either way, we should be able to trace the murderer."

She nodded. "I'd better find my DS."

"Okay. If you need me again, I'll be over at the vehicles."

"Thanks." She gave him a smile, before heading after Dewi.

∽

THE ROOM WAS silent as Yvonne began the morning briefing.

"We haven't found dental records to match those of our Jane Doe." Her eyes passed along the rows of plain and uniformed officers, taking in their worried faces and stiff shoulders. "There are other options available and, soon, there'll be a facial reconstruction. That, and the clothes, should stir memories in friends and family. We need maximum public engagement with this enquiry."

She pointed to the photographs on the board. "Our Jane Doe was underground for three years. We have the grave site. What we don't know is who the killer is, and why he exhumed her, leaving her on display forty miles from where he buried her. Lots of unknowns, but we are not without leads. West Mercia are doing door-to-door enquires, in Bishop's Castle and Church Stretton, and scouring their mis per lists."

She scrawled salient points on the board. "As soon as we have a face, there'll be a national appeal for information."

Following the briefing, she phoned Hanson to make an appointment with his intriguing anthropologist.

∼

WYN ANSWERED HER KNOCK, his blonde hair damp from the shower, fingernails bearing traces of reddish-brown clay. A matchstick protruded from his lips. He toggled it with his teeth, his eyes exploring her face. He removed it before greeting her.

"DI Giles. Come. Hope it doesn't frighten you." He cleared his throat, moving back.

"Thanks. I can't wait to see her." Yvonne edged into the airy studio where two long tables ran parallel. The generous space between, enabled ample access.

Lining the walls, shelves sported various-sized pots, brushes and tools, including scrapers.

A short pole held the head on the table to her left.

"I'm modelling facial muscles." Wyn smoothed clay over the teeth with his thumbs

She watched him develop the right thickness, guided by pins projecting from the skull surface, kneading until satisfied it was right.

Like a face with the skin peeled. She shuddered, thinking of the killer who had stripped the remains of their flesh. The reverse of this reconstruction.

"What do you think so far?" He stepped away from the head.

"I'm impressed. Though I still can't picture the girl."

"Early days." He smiled. "I've developed the rough shape, using standard muscle thickness. Soon, the upper layers of fat and skin will be on and the finer detail applied.

Then you'll view the face of your victim. Or, at least, enough likeness to jog the memories of her loved ones."

Yvonne shook his hand. "Great work, I can't wait to see it finished."

"I'll let you know."

3

NICOLE BENOIT

A relentless, mid-July sun continued the heatwave which had revealed so many patterns in the fields. Brown lines of previous structures. Previous times. Previous lives.

Nicole Benoit lifted both feet off the pedals and freewheeled down the hill. The rush of air was a joy. Her bun allowed stray red tendrils to tickle her face and neck. She beamed, her eyes ablaze. This was freedom. This was life.

He took a right turn off the track below and stopped. She watched him alight from his bicycle and lay it on the ground next to him, along with his backpack. He extracted a large picnic basket from the rack at the back.

She applied her brakes, in danger of overshooting the turn. The sudden stop almost unseated her. Her chest heaved, and she sat for a few moments regaining her breath.

"This is a good spot." He turned his handsome head towards her and waved his hand around, showing a well-grazed area, separating two mounds of heather.

She nodded, breathing fast. "It's beautiful up here. This was a *good choice."* She was more aware of her Languedoc accent when she talked to him. She blushed, casting her eyes downwards.

He pulled out a chequered cloth and placed it on the ground, proceeding to position plates and cutlery onto it.

She approached the sandwiches, grapes, cheese and biscuits, he laid out on plates..

"This looks so good. This was a lot of trouble. I feel spoiled." She was smiling again, taking a seat at one end of the cloth.

He returned her warmth. "Who wouldn't want to spoil you?"

Her eyes met his. There was something in his gaze. Something she couldn't quite put her finger on.

~

THEY ATE IN RELATIVE SILENCE, *both lost in the quiet beauty of the place. There wasn't another soul around. Her hunger surprised her. His food tasted of summer heaven.*

After they had eaten their fill, she gathered the plates and cutlery, preparing them to go back into the basket.

She went to speak and saw him hide something behind his back, but not before she had spied the corner of a jewellery box. She held her breath. They'd known each other a few months. He wouldn't propose? Would he?

The more she thought about it, the more obvious it became. The bike ride, the picnic, this beautiful spot at Carding Mill. All of it leading up to something.

His eyes on her face, she coloured again.

He brought his hands from behind his back, producing a blue velvet box. It was long. A little too long. Knots formed in her chest.

She felt silly, hiding her mouth behind her hand. Had he seen the confusion in her eyes?

"What have I done to deserve this?" She held up a gold chain, on the end of which was a locket with an intricate flower design.

She looked at him through long lashes and stray tendrils of hair.

"I saw it and thought of you." He kept his eyes on her face, his expression enigmatic.

"Thank you."

"I thought you'd like it."

She leaned to kiss his forehead.

Without warning, he clambered back onto his bike and rode off.

"Wait!" She clamoured to get on her own and follow him, scraping the backs of her calves with the pedals as she scrambled to get going.

He raced away, out of Carding Mill and toward the Long Mynd.

"Oh... merde!"

∼

SHE CYCLED ALONGSIDE THE STREAM, approaching the National Trust coffee shop. On her left, cars lined the route and small children played in the stream, their parents chatting on the benches or else taking a stroll down the road.

She couldn't see her companion anywhere and questioned whether he had come this way at all. A few thousand yards further, she found his bike tethered in the upper car park, just before the track which meandered up and out of the valley.

She giggled, hearing a sound in the trees to her left. He was playing hide-and-seek.

She leaned her bike against the fence, securing it with a bike lock, and headed on foot towards the sound. "Hello? Hello?"

She didn't notice the crossbow levelled at her, nor the

watchful figure waiting for the right moment. The takedown was swift. She made no sound, save that of her body hitting foliage.

∽

YVONNE STARED at the finished head. Wyn had done a remarkable job. His attention to detail astonished her. The red of the hair, reflected in the long, delicate eyelashes. He'd emphasised the high cheekbones and slender nose by holding the hair off the face, in a ponytail. Amber eyes followed the detective round the room. Wyn had given the girl new life, and she was beautiful.

"What do you think?" Wyn tilted his head to the side, his eyes on the Yvonne's face.

"Amazing." She closed the few yards between herself and the likeness. "She has such grace and dignity. How did you get the skin pores? They look real."

He walked to his tools and held up a cloth. "Leather." He grabbed leftover clay and placed the leather on top. "I lay this against the skin and stroke. Pull it away and there you go." He gave her the clay to examine.

"Incredible." She ran her hands over it. "The extra touches bring this girl so vividly back to life."

"So long as it helps to solve her murder." Wyn rubbed his chin. "I've kind of grown close to her over the last few weeks."

Yvonne reached out. "May I?"

"Be my guest."

Yvonne placed a hand each side of the young girl's face, her thumbs brushed the eyebrows. "She's almost real."

"If only she could talk to you." Wyn gave a wry smile, his eyelids lowered. His gaze was on the DI's neck and shoulders.

"I wish she could." She sighed, removing her hands from the head with reverent care.

"She would tell you the name of her murderer."

"And tell us of the dreams that died with her. Such a waste." She closed her eyes and whispered, "I *will* find your killer. I promise."

"The job is in good hands." He said, placing with a match between his teeth.

The words reminded her where she was. "You've done such a good job, Wyn. We'll bring it to national attention and then it's a case of fingers crossed that someone recognises her. But," she turned back to the likeness. "I am *certain* they will."

∽

THEIR DEDICATED PHONE line was ringing off the hook. They had three names, so far. One of them kept coming up.

"Nicole Benoit." Callum handed Yvonne a file. "It's all in there. Nicole vanished three years ago."

"Three years ago." Yvonne flicked through the notes and photographs..

"She was a nineteen-year-old student from the Languedoc in France. Spoke good English and was about half-way though a course in Business Studies. She was over here on a three-month exchange visit and had was staying with an English couple near Church Stretton." Callum checked his pocketbook. "Frank and Elizabeth Whately. Also living with them was their twenty-two-year-old son, Stephen."

"Good work, Callum." Yvonne stared at the photograph of Nicole, holding her breath.

"Ma'am?"

"Sorry, Callum. I can't get over how much she looks like Wyn's reconstruction. She could have modelled for him."

Callum nodded. "I knew as soon as I found that photo, she was our girl."

"Where's Dewi?"

"I think he's still on the phone, ma'am."

"Do me a favour and ask him to meet me at my office? I will telephone the Whatelys and see if they'll agree to us paying them a visit today."

"Will do."

"Oh, and, Callum? Can you chase down Nicole's dental records from the France? Hanson is already on it but I'd like to have incontrovertible evidence for the match. We should also inform Nicole's parents of what is happening."

"Yes, ma'am."

∾

Dewi parked on the lane outside Spring Cottage on the outskirts of Church Stretton.

Yvonne straightened her skirt, wishing she'd ironed it. Meeting Nicole's friends in crumpled clothing felt disrespectful.

"Ready?" Dewi was at her side. His shirt, most definitely pressed, probably by his wife.

She nodded. "Nice tie."

"Thanks."

They walked the couple of hundred yards to the cream cottage with the stained oak door. Dewi rang the bell.

A middle-aged female answered, her hair in a neatly coiffed bun and sleeves rolled up to the elbows. A streak of white smeared her cheek and the rich smell of baking greeted them.

"You'd better come in," she said, after Dewi introduced them. "My husband is in the study." She led them through the narrow hallway, next to the stairs.

"We'll speak to you both, if that's okay." Yvonne's voice was soft, but Elizabeth Whately turned her face away as though she would prefer to not get involved.

The four of them settled on the three-piece, in the sitting room, the detectives positioned next to wood burner. Yvonne removed her jacket and cleared her throat. "Thank you for seeing us today. Did you hear the news last night?"

Elizabeth's gaze shot to her husband. She clasped one hand with the other, chewing her cheek.

"What news?" Frank Whately, small and stocky, stretched his legs in front of him.

Yvonne flicked through her notebook. "Do you remember the young student Nicole Benoit?"

Again, Sheila's glanced towards her husband.

"Yes. She stayed with us a few years ago. Left in a hurry." Frank reclined in his seat, hands on his ample stomach.

"They logged her as a missing person, Mr Whate*ly*. She didn't leave, she vanished." Yvonne resisted the temptation to raise her voice.

"I always assumed she'd run off with a boyfriend. She was popular with the men."

"Can you tell me which men?"

"What is this?" Frank pulled his legs back in.

"Mr and Mrs Whately, I'm sorry to inform you, we found Nicole's remains two weeks ago."

Elizabeth's hands flew to her mouth.

"Someone murdered her and we think it happened near here."

Frank leaned towards them. "Murdered? I can't believe it." Hands on head, he puffed his cheeks out. "When she went, we wondered if something bad might have happened to her, but we hoped she'd run off with someone. We've always had students. Occasionally, they get homesick and leave early. But... murdered?" He clicked his tongue. "Well, I'll be... Poor kid."

"You said she had male friends-"

The door bell rang several times. Someone was impatient to come in.

"Liz, can you get that?" Frank ran a hand through his hair and loosened the top of his shirt.

Liz rose from her seat and disappeared along the hallway.

Yvonne listened.

"Mum, they've found Nicole. They've-" A male voice gushed.

"Stephen, the police are here."

"Oh." Stephen stopped talking. He and his mum joined them in the sitting room.

"This is our boy, Stephen." Frank frowned at his son. "He runs a book store in the town."

Stephen wasn't making eye contact, his lank hair covered half his face like a curtain. It was difficult to follow his expressions. Yvonne estimated him to be around six-feet-one. Dark haired, he would have been handsome if he wasn't so shy.

Stephen leaned his elbows on his knees. "I saw the news." His eyes swung from Yvonne to Dewi and back. "Someone killed her."

"Yes." The DI nodded.

"Any idea who?" He pushed his hands deep into his trouser pockets.

"Not yet. We had hoped you might have ideas."

"Who, me?"

"Any of you. Did you know her? Stephen?"

"Oh. Oh, yes." His words tumbled over themselves.

"Were you close?"

"Me and Nicole? No. Well, yes, in a way. We were friends. Just friends." He nodded to emphasise his words.

Frank grunted. "We hadn't known her long, Inspector. She'd only been with us six weeks. We've had lots of students, over the years."

Yvonne turned her full attention back to Frank. "You mentioned male friends. Can you give us names?"

"Well, I…" Frank rubbed his forehead. "Maynard was one. Can't remember his first name."

"Craig." Stephen offered. "Craig Maynard. He's a teacher."

"He teaches at Church Stretton School," Frank clarified.

"Thank you. Who else? Can you remember?"

"Terry. Terry Mason. He works behind the bar in the Kings Arms. He's friends with Stephen." Frank looked at his son.

"Anyone else?" Yvonne looked from Frank to Stephen and back.

Both shook their heads.

"Do you remember much of the day Nicole disappeared?"

"She took her bike around eleven-ish in the morning. She never returned." Frank shook his head.

"Was the bike found?"

"No."

"Did she say where she was going?"

"No. And we never asked. She was free to come and go as she pleased, provided she was in by ten o'clock."

"Did she have her mobile with her?"

"She didn't have one."

Yvonne's eyes narrowed. "No mobile phone?"

Frank shook his head. "She said she didn't want them. She said they stopped people living their lives. Stopped them living in-the-moment."

Yvonne nodded. "She had a point. Unusual, though. Did she ever call home?"

"She called her parents every Sunday from our house phone." Liz Whately, silent until now, pointed towards the phone on the bookcase. "She phoned them on the morning she vanished."

"Were the phone calls normal? Did she argue with anyone on those calls?"

She shook her head. "She always seemed happy after talking to them. She missed her family."

"I have one more question for Stephen."

Stephen shifted the weight between his feet.

"Where were you, the Friday before last?"

Stephen looked at her, for the first time, opened mouthed. "Why?"

"Someone moved Nicole's remains and left in public."

Stephen looked at his mum. "I was home in my flat, in Church Stretton."

"Can anyone verify that?"

"Is he a suspect, now?" Frank's frown deepened.

"Everyone who knew her is a suspect until we rule them out."

Stephen shook his head. "Don't think so. I was tired after work, I had a bath and watched TV after my dinner. Then, bed."

"You didn't socialise?"

"I don't go out much."

"I see." Yvonne rose from her seat, followed by Dewi.

"Thank you all for talking to us." She smiled at each of them. "I will speak with you again."

∽

"Is it me, or was that strange?" Dewi pulled a face.

Yvonne shook her head. "I don't know. People react in odd ways, to shock and grief, but I see what you mean. I think they know more than they are saying. Something was bothering Liz. I'd like talk to her, alone. We need to locate Craig Maynard and Terry Mason."

4
CONNECTIONS

"Will Tozer."

Yvonne took a deep breath. "Hi, Will. It's Yvonne Giles, Dyfed-Powys-"

"Yvonne, I was just about to ring you. I'm sorry I couldn't be with you to interview the Whatelys the other day. We've been flat out dealing with County Lines. Drug squad needed our help."

"You too?" Yvonne sighed. "I've lost my DS this week for the same reason. They're raiding every couple of weeks, at the moment."

He clicked his tongue. "Vital work. Anyway, how can I help?"

"There's a couple more people I'd like to speak to about Nicole Benoit's murder. They live and work in Church Stretton. I don't want to tread on your toes but I think they may have vital information."

"Can I interview with you?"

"That would be helpful since, like I say, I don't have my DS with me this week."

"Who we talking about?"

"Craig Maynard, English teacher and Terry Mason, who works as a barman in Houseman's bar in the town."

"I know Terry," Tozer affirmed. "I don't know Maynard, but I know *of* him. He works at Church Stretton School. He teaches my niece."

"I could see them both today, if you're available. Or, at least, Craig Maynard."

"I'll ring the school and set it up. I'll call you back."

Yvonne was about to thank him, but the dead tone stopped her in her tracks. Tozer had gone.

∼

SHE PARKED in the car park at Church Stretton School, on Shrewsbury Road, waiting for Will to join her. She leaned on her car, scanning her surroundings

The school sign bore the mission statement, 'Achievement for all'. She pondered this as a Honda Civic pulled into the car park and straight into a park space. One smooth movement.

Will Tozer jumped out and waved.

She loved his enthusiasm, chatting to him with ease as they made their way into the school.

Maynard had agreed to speak with them on his rest break, a secretary told them through a hatch, file under one arm and a sheaf of papers under the opposite. She sighed, placing them on her desk, before escorting the detectives to an empty classroom where she asked them to wait. Will agreed to a coffee. Yvonne requested water.

Craig Maynard walked in without knocking. His brown hair, tousled. He carried an arm full of exercise books which he set down on the top of a desk, taking off his tweed jacket to deposit it on the back of the chair.

As he started towards them, his hip caught the pile of books. They cascaded in chaos to the floor.

Yvonne ran to help him pick them up, feeling guilty for taking up his rest time. "Thank you for agreeing to speak with us."

"You mean I had a choice?"

She noticed patches of damp under each of his arms. "We wanted to talk with you about a former friend of yours."

He frowned at her. "*Former* friend?"

"Nicole Benoit."

He drew in a sharp breath. "Nicole? You found her? Is she okay?"

"We found her." Yvonne nodded. "But, she's not okay."

He shook his head, his mouth open. "I don't understand."

Tozer pulled a face. "Didn't you see the news yesterday? Or this morning?"

"I was out last night. I didn't see the news."

"No newspapers?"

"Not until the weekend."

Yvonne accepted her water from the secretary, turning back to Craig. "Mr Maynard, Nicole is dead."

He stopped what he was doing. "Dead? How?"

"Murdered." Yvonne refrained from giving further detail.

"But who? Wait, wait a minute. You think it involved me? Is that why you're here?"

Yvonne shook her head. "We're finding out more about her. How she spent her time. The best people to tell us are her friends. I understand you were one?"

"We were close." He looked at his shoes. "I'm still trying to get my head around the fact she's dead."

"We can give you a few minutes if you like?"

He shook his head. "No. No, it's all right. Dead?"

"Yes. We think she most likely died on or soon after the day she vanished."

His face was grey.

"Are you sure you wouldn't like a few minutes?"

He shook his head.

"Thank you. She was on a student exchange, right?"

"She planned to teach geography after she qualified." He shook his head. "She was so full of life."

"How did you meet?"

"She wanted to improve her English, though it was already decent. I had placed ads in the local newspapers and shops windows. I offered extra-curricular English lessons, aimed at school pupils who needed extra help for upcoming exams."

"And Nicole answered your ad?"

"Yes. She phoned me up and asked if I would consider giving her English tuition and I agreed. Snapped her hand off, actually. I needed the money."

"And you became friends?"

"We were close."

"Did you have a relationship?"

"Yes, but not with Nicole. I was seeing someone else, Rose Wilson. This was before we got married. She worked in the library in Church Stretton."

"I see. Did Nicole ever want *more* than friendship?"

He shook his head. "No. Never."

His eyes flickered as though he wasn't sure, or he was being dishonest about their relationship.

"Was Nicole seeing anyone else?"

"Not that I know of. She had friends but no-one that close. I mean, there was Stephen Whately. She spent time with him and Terry from The Kings Arms."

"What about female friends? Did she have a best friend?"

He hesitated, shifting in his seat. "Rosie. She was friends with Rosie."

Yvonne glanced at her notes. "Was that Rose Wilson, your wife?"

He cleared his throat. "Yes."

The bell clamoured above them and Yvonne jumped. Her heart hammered in her chest.

"I have to go." He stood up. "Next lesson starts in five."

Yvonne nodded. She and Tozer rose from their seats. "Thank you for your time. We'll let you know if we need to speak to you again. Please call us of you think of anything relevant."

∾

She gave the doorbell two pokes. His flat was on the second floor. She detected music coming from an open window. He hadn't heard her. She poked the bell again and this time the sound of feet followed, hitting the stairs. She smiled.

"Sorry. Sorry." He appeared on the doorstep, pushing his wayward hair back with his hand and squeezing himself against the wall to allow her to pass. His feet were bare. "I lost track of the time."

She grimaced and looked at her watch.

"Don't worry." He checked his. "I'll add an extra fifteen minutes onto the end of the session. If that's okay with you?"

She nodded. "I would like that. Merci."

He was easy to be with. They sat on the floor, surrounded by books and notes. He referred to them at intervals, illustrating his points. She studied his profile. Like an artist, creating a charcoal study for a masterpiece, she would begin at his hairline and end at the strong jawline.

More than once, he caught her looking. His eyes would linger on her, only to return to the passage they were working on.

She wondered what he was thinking.

∼

IN THE KINGS ARMS on High Street, lunch was winding down. Staff scurried back and forth, clearing away dishes and seeing to thirsty punters at the bar.

Yvonne and DS Tozer split up. She headed to a table in the corner of the main room and Tozer proceeded towards the bar to check in with the proprietor.

Wood-clad walls, stone floors and beamed ceilings gave the long room an intimate atmosphere. Terry Mason had agreed to speak to the officers on his break.

A blonde-haired, broad-shouldered young man in his mid-twenties, carried a pile of plates and cutlery. She wondered if that was Terry. He shot her a quick glance, his face flushed, shirt coming out of his trousers.

She smiled and nodded, to let him know it was okay. He could finish what he was doing.

Tozer was busy eyeing a pint of ale on the bar and licking his lips. Yvonne couldn't make out the conversation he was having with the owner, but Tozer held his hands up, shaking his head. She guessed he'd refused the pint.

The DI kicked off her shoes beneath the table and placed her feet on the cold stone tiles. It felt good. She closed her eyes.

"Sorry about that."

She opened them.

The blonde seated himself opposite her. "Terry. Terry

Mason. You're from the police?" His voice was deeper than she'd expected.

"Yes. I'm DI Giles." She pointed to the bar. "That is DS Tozer. We're here to talk to you about Nicole Benoit."

Terry looked at the table. The corners of his mouth turned down. "I heard." He shook his head. "I can't believe it."

"I'm sorry." Yvonne gave him a moment before continuing. "We're trying to understand who she was and what she was doing in the weeks leading up to her death. You may have information which could help us."

He looked at her, his eyes wandering her face. "*Anything* I can do to help."

Will Tozer joined them at the table, carrying three orange juices.

Yvonne smiled at the DS and continued. "How did you and Nicole meet?"

Mason glazed over in a thousand-yard stare. "She liked live music." He shuddered, as though his breath were a sob, and sighed. "Loved. She *loved* live music, especially blues. We met at a local gig. I like blues, too."

"Were you close?" Tozer pushed a juice towards Terry.

Terry turned his attention to the DS. "I didn't kill her." He ignored the juice.

"I didn't say you did." Tozer's eyes narrowed.

Yvonne kept her voice soft. "You cared about her, didn't you?"

Terry turned back to her. "I think I loved her."

"You think?" Tozer raised his eyebrows.

Terry cleared his throat. "I loved her. But, when I look back, I'd only known her a few weeks. That's not long enough, is it? Not long enough to know someone."

"What did you love about her?" Yvonne took a sip of her juice.

"She was beautiful. I loved the way she moved. The way she smiled. The way she tossed her hair. Everything. It obsessed me. From the night I met her, I couldn't get her out of my head. I had a few sleepless nights, I can tell you."

"Did she return your feelings?"

"I don't know. I didn't get around to asking her."

"But you were close?"

"Yes."

"When did you notice her disappearance?"

"Early on. I had a call from Craig, to say she'd gone missing and to ask if I'd seen her."

"Was that Craig Maynard?"

"Er, yes."

"And had you?"

"What? Seen her? No." He pursed his lips and avoided eye contact.

"You hadn't seen her that day?"

"No, and I didn't seen her the day before."

"Can you remember which day you received the phone call?"

"No. I remember that it was when the police made enquires, so it must have been the day after someone first reported her missing."

Yvonne placed one of her cards on the table and pushed it towards Terry. "If you remember anything else, Terry, I want you to call me on that number. Will you do that?"

"Sure." Terry nodded and shot a glance back towards the bar.

"It's okay, we won't keep you any longer." She rose from her seat. "Thank you for your help."

~

"*He does my head in.*"

"Who?"

"Craig."

"What has he done, now?" Nicole giggled, accepting the offered glass of wine.

Rose plumped on the white-leather couch with an exaggerated sigh. "Work, work, work. That's all I ever hear. I mean, his job *is* important." She ran a hand through her platinum curls. "He's too young to stay in and so *am* I."

"Go out with me." She settled next to her friend.

"Oh, I love going out with others, I do. It's just... well-"

"It's okay. I understand." Nicole touched her friend's arm. "Remember the things you like about him." She gazed around the open-plan lounge and kitchen. "He does the housework. This place is stunning. Look at the sparkle on that." She pointed to the granite countertop.

"Yeah. He does that."

"And he surprises you with... how do you say... gifts?"

"Yeah." Rose grimaced.

"Cooks dinner-"

"All right. All right." Rose laughed, pushing her friend. "You made your point. I'm an ungrateful cow."

Nicole shrugged. "Talk to him. Tell him how you feel. If he doesn't know, he won't change."

Rose curled her nose. "Can't you come *every* time I have a crisis?"

"I'm not available twenty-four-seven." Nicole grinned and received a friendly slap for her cheek.

~

THE BAR GOT BUSIER *by the moment.*

The lead singer adjusted his ponytail before tapping the microphone. "One, two, testing... One, two." A scowl creased his forehead as he struggled to hear. He signalled to his sound engineer to up the volume. The rest of his band appeared oblivious, fiddling with their instruments and playing a few notes here and there. Turning knobs on their amplifiers. Some minutes later, the whole band struck up.

Nicole took a sip from her half-pint of lager, her eyes wandering the room. Her friend, Rose, had told her Madison Blues was a popular band and they would have to turn away some people. She had made sure she arrived early. She tapped her foot to the beat. Even the sound check had people tapping their feet and swaying.

A few feet away from her, a well-built, blonde young man was also tapping his foot and swaying to the song. He took off his jacket and set it down on the table behind. The hair at his temples was damp. He caught her looking. Nicole coloured, turning her attention back to the band.

Within moments he was at her shoulder. "Hi. Have you seen this band before? They're superb."

Nicole shook her head. "No. Never. But my friends told me they rock."

"I'm Terry." He held out his hand.

Nicole accepted the handshake and smiled, her lids lowered. She shifted her weight from one foot to the other. "Nicole."

He leaned his head to one side. "French?"

"Oui. Er, Yes. I'm here to study English."

"Love your accent." A smile filled his face. Dark eyes, glistening.

Nicole liked him. "Thank you. I like yours, too."

"Do you mind if I join you?"

"No. Be my guest."

"Your English is great."

"Excuse me?"

He put his mouth closer to her ear. "Your English. It's great."

"Ah, thank you. Perhaps you should tell my tutor."

He laughed. "Perhaps, I will."

He was easy to be with. In between songs they snatched a few bits of conversation and he insisted on buying her a second lager. However, when he placed a hand in the middle of her back, she stiffened and he removed it again.

5

FREINDS REUNITED

Tasha's eyes sparkled as she eyed her plate of food. "To what do I owe this pleasure?" She looked up at Yvonne, as the waitress in 'La Traviatta' Italian restaurant, on Park Street, poured their water.

"I thought we were due a catch up." Yvonne grinned. "Do I need an ulterior motive?"

Tasha laughed. "No, but I sense something..."

Yvonne smiled. "I *have* missed you. But, you are right. As usual. I'm working another murder case and would appreciate your input."

"Official or unofficial help?"

"Unofficial, but I could speak with the DCI. It depends where the case is heading."

Yvonne outlined what had occurred as regards Nicole Benoit's disappearance and her remains being found.

"I remember." Tasha pursed her lips. "I remember when that girl went missing. It made the national headlines."

Yvonne nodded. "And, no word from that time until a few weeks ago when we found her skeleton, re-articulated and leaning against the gate of a field."

"And you're saying that the person who put her there, left clues to how she died."

"It's the most bizarre thing I have ever witnessed, in all my years in the force."

Tasha nodded. "It's a first for me." She sat back in her chair. "You said someone cleaned the bones?"

"Yes. There was staining but, in terms of flesh etc, they were clean."

"It would have taken a long time to clean and then thread every piece of bone together. Days, or even weeks."

"Who does that?" Yvonne sighed.

"You think whoever did it was her killer?"

"I think he has to be the killer or someone close to the killer. I mean, they had buried her on the Long Mynd. It looked very much like they intended it to be forever. Her body was in an unmarked grave, in a desolate spot, until a few weeks ago. Whoever unearthed her had to have known about her murder. It's not somewhere you would h*appen* upon a grave."

Tasha nodded, as she finished chewing. "Would I be able to look?"

"Sure. It would give you a better idea of what I am talking about."

"Great. Just let me know when you're planning an outing and I'll try to fit in."

Yvonne jumped as someone tapped her on the shoulder.

"Wyn." She turned to stare at him, wide-eyed.

He smiled, and scratched the top of his chest, where his collarless, white linen shirt was open at the neck. "I wanted to give this restaurant a try. Didn't fancy the evening meal at the bed-and-breakfast. Fancy seeing *you* here."

Yvonne stood. "Tasha, this is Wyn Sealander. He's been working with us this past few weeks. He helped us identify

Nicole's remains by reconstructing her face. Wyn, this is my friend, Dr. Natasha Phillips. She's a criminal psychologist."

"Pleased to meet you." He held out his hand and Tasha shook it, nodding at him.

"Are you meeting anyone here?" Yvonne asked as she returned to her chair. "You're welcome to join us."

Wyn glanced at Tasha and held a hand up. "Thanks, but I can see you're busy. Besides, I'm tired. I will disappear into a corner and sleep while I eat."

Tasha cleared her throat.

"Oh. Okay. Well, enjoy your meal." Yvonne raised her eyebrows at Tasha after he had gone.

Tasha shrugged. "I've no idea."

"Did you put him off?" Yvonne laughed.

Tasha shook her head. "No."

∼

CARS DOTTED the lay-bys adjoining the stream. Although early in the season, tourism was already hotting up for Carding Mill Valley and the Long Mynd. The area was popular for families with small children. The latter appeared to be spending most of their time paddling the stream in their wellies.

Yvonne parked in the first available spot, next to the National Trust cafe, where she and Tasha planned to have lunch. She stretched towards the sky. A sunny, first Saturday in May. The temperature, a welcome eighteen degrees. Work and pleasure.

Both women wore walking gear for the one-and-a-half-hour trek up to Pole Bank, the highest point on the Long Mynd. Nicole's makeshift grave had been between Pole Bank and the place known as Boiling Well and Tasha wanted to see it for herself. The circuitous route would take them back to the cafe and lunch.

Tasha shouldered her rucksack and helped the DI on with hers. "What have you got in there, Yvonne?" she asked, as she heaved it up.

"Two litres of water, a camera, my notebooks, iPad and spare clothing." Yvonne grinned. "Too much?"

Tasha laughed. "We're walking ten miles, not climbing Mount Everest."

Yvonne pulled a face. She took a folded map from her trouser pocket. "Okay, we're here." She pointed to the cafe and toilet symbol. "We should follow the stream, taking the trackway past the top car park to the head of Carding Mill Valley, then take the right. When we meet the fork, we follow Mott's Road up the Hill. We'll look at the map when we get to the fork."

"Sounds good."

Yvonne grimaced. "Sorry, Tasha. Could you grab my camera from my bag?"

Tasha fished it out, and the DI put her head through the strap. "Good to go. Thank you, Tasha."

They walk up past the top car park. The track wound up through the valley. The hills served as a colourful back drop, with trees and small shrubs adding interest and a sense of balance.

Tasha took deep breaths, turning now and then to gaze at the valley below.

Yvonne's thoughts were on Nicole and whether the young woman had walked this pathway on the day she died.

When they reached the fork in the tracks, they took the right and headed along Mott's Road.

"Wow." Tasha said, as she turned to look behind them.

"I think Nicole came up here the day she died." Yvonne took in the view with Tasha.

"I agree. It's a long way to carry a body uphill."

"I think it's likely she knew her murderer and met him here."

"How far is the grave from here?" Tasha asked, stopping, her breathing laboured.

"A mile, maybe," Yvonne answered, examining the small map.

Tasha pulled a face.

"It's not *all* up hill," Yvonne reassured.

∽

They could not see the figure stretched out amongst the heathers, high on Calf Ridge, to their left, binoculars in hand. The figure who had watched them from the moment they parked the car. The figure who would continue to follow and watch them as they made their way along Portway and on up the hill to Pole Bank.

∽

"This is it. The highest point of the Long Mynd." Yvonne checked her map once more. "You can see both the Brecon Beacons and the Malvern Hills." She showed the relevant directions. "And *there* is where he buried her." She pointed down to the place near Boiling Well. It was still an open wound on the landscape, bordered by police tape and various markers.

"So, given the terrain, he or she killed Nicole around here, somewhere." Tasha turned in circles, examining the landscape. "I wonder if he was watching her before he killed her."

"You mean spying on her? Like stalking?"

"Well, let's face it. There's no shortage of vantage points."

Yvonne nodded. "Which makes it as likely to be a stranger-murder as it was someone she knew?"

"Has anyone else disappeared from this area?" Tasha turned her gaze back to the DI.

"Dai and Callum are checking other cases. So far, nothing for this specific area."

"Can I have a peek at the case file this week?" Tasha rubbed her chin.

"I'll speak with the DCI on Monday."

Tasha wandered around the perimeter of the grave and continued to peruse the surroundings, steeped in her own thoughts.

6

TROUBLE AND STRIFE

Rosie glared at her husband. "*When* did the police talk to you about Nicole?"

Craig threw down his bag, loosening his tie and running a hand through his already dishevelled hair. "A few days ago. They came to the school."

"What did you tell them?" Rosie rolled her sleeves up, glasses pushed onto the top of her head. Rigid.

"Well, there wasn't a lot I could tell them, except what I knew."

"Did you tell them you were seeing her behind my back? Did you tell them that?" Rosie reached behind, grabbing a plate from the breakfast bar and hurling it at her husband.

He ducked in time. The plate smashed against the wall. The pieces rebounding onto his head and neck. "I wasn't seeing her behind your back."

Another plate.

"Rosie. Rosie, Stop!"

Another plate. "First, you were home all the time. Then, you were out a lot. I found that note in the drawer you keep locked. The *'see you later'* note. A note you seemed desperate to hide."

Craig shook his head. "That note was innocent. She left because she hadn't been able to keep our earlier session. It wasn't what you thought. We've been through all this. Hell, even *if* I had wanted to have an affair with her, Nicole just wasn't a loose girl. For God's sake, she was *your* best friend."

"Was she?" Rosie glowered in his direction, but her eyes did not focus. She was somewhere else. A different time. "All the extra tuition. Did she need it? Or, did you?"

"Rosie, we were engaged-"

"What?" Rosie pulled a face. "We didn't get engaged until two months after she disappeared. Is that what you told the police? That we were engaged at the time?"

He stopped crouching, slowly coming to his full height. "It's been a long time. I forget the order of things."

Rosie grunted. "Well, that's convenient."

"It's true." He stood, hunched over, staring at his shoes.

"Did you tell them the truth about where you were, the day she disappeared? You had told them you were with me. Got me to lie for you. But, you weren't with me, were you?"

"You know what happened. We argued, again. I had to cool off."

"With Nicole."

" Not with Nicole. Alone. Rosie, for heaven's sake, just stop. You need help." He looked straight into Rosie's eyes. "What if *you* saw her after our argument?"

"What?"

"*You* could have killed her."

"Don't be ridiculous." Rosie shook her head, her pupils so large, her eyes appeared black.

"You found the note, got mad, and killed her."

"Really? How did I get her body up the Long Mynd to bury her? Hm?"

"Maybe you killed her up there?"

Rosie made a move towards the rest of the plates.

Craig ran for the door.

~

"I'm glad she has a name." Tasha put her head level with Wyn's model of Nicole. "Can I touch?"

"Sure." Wyn perched himself on a nearby stool, wiggling his toes. "Be my guest."

He was barefoot. Yvonne stared, surprised that she hadn't noticed it before. She stood at the back of the studio, giving them room.

Wyn leaned against the wall, cool and casual. "Are you any nearer to finding her killer?" he asked, looking in Tasha's direction.

"No." Yvonne shook her head, forcing her eyes from his toes' soft hair. "We're still examining her close associates. Tasha is working on a profile for us. This could be a stranger-murder."

Wyn nodded. "Sure."

Tasha gazed at the model. "She has an open countenance... Trusting."

"Are you getting vibes?" Yvonne tilted her head to one side as she tried to read Tasha's thoughts.

The psychologist returned to the DI's side. "I'll finish reading the file and I'll have a workable profile for you within twenty-four hours."

"That's great." Yvonne waited for more, but nothing came.

Instead, they thanked Wyn and walked to their cars in

relative silence. The DI thought better of quizzing her friend but Tasha was still concentrating.

˷

TRUE TO HER WORD, Tasha was back at Newtown station the following day with her profile of the killer.

Yvonne greeted her with good news. "The DCI says we can pay you for your help. West Mercia force have agreed to contribute a portion."

"That's fantastic, Yvonne. Thank you." Tasha gave the DI a broad smile, but the smile faded. "You've hit the headlines, by the way." Tasha placed a copy of the County Times on the desk.

"What?" Yvonne picked up the paper.

'Lead detective digs deep, but not deep enough' the headline ran. Underneath, a photograph of Yvonne and Tasha at the open grave on the Long Mynd, fronted by police tape. The article, itself was not complimentary regarding the lack of news and slow progress of the investigation. It included comments from locals, who spoke of their horror and how they couldn't sleep at night. A killer was on the loose and the police were tight-lipped.

Yvonne looked up. "The DCI has scheduled a press conference tomorrow. That will help reassure the locals. We're doing everything we can. They need to know that."

Tasha nodded. "I know. I have the profile. Would you like to hear it?"

"I can't wait."

˷

TASHA TALKED Yvonne and her team through the details.

"I believe the person who disinterred Nicole's remains, putting them on display, was the same person who killed her. The intimacy of exhuming her body, polishing the bones and piecing them back together, suggests the unsub was likely someone she knew. Either that, or it was a stranger who had stalked her for some time and knew her through his obsession with her. I further suspect there will be other victims.

"I think the killer is likely male and a loner, with artistic leanings. He may be a painter or photographer, but unlikely to be an abstract artist. His work will be meticulous.

"He'll be somewhere in his mid-twenties to mid-thirties and fit. Likely bullied in school, he had a strict father and an overbearing or absent mother. He needs to control the things he possesses and the people he loves. Everything he does or achieves is art."

She continued. "Explore disappearances over the last few years. This guy has a type, and we should examine whether there were other victims. That's as far as I can go with the limited information given me. I hope it helps."

"How many more could we be talking about?" Dewi scratched his head, his face drawn.

"Hard to say." Tasha folded her arms. "Not that many, though. I suspect he's still early in his career."

"Are we likely to see more dressed skeletons turning up on our lanes, then?" Callum placed his hands on his head, with a sigh.

Tasha nodded. "If he has killed others, it's likely he will display *them*, too. A lot depends on his motivation for putting the remains out there. The killing, and articulation of the bones, are about the relationship with the victim, real or imagined. Placing them on display is about the wider community. He's saying, 'Look at me. Look at what I can do.

Be afraid.' And he's taunting you, the police. 'I did this and you won't catch me'. It's possible, he became frustrated that no-one was looking for him. The excavation was an attention-seeking move."

"It was still an open case..." Yvonne frowned.

"Yes, but there's a difference between an open case, and an active incident room."

The place buzzed with the team's chatter. The energy in CID was palpable.

"Thank you for that." Yvonne gave her friend a hug. "It's given us something to work with. It's energised my team and we can produce some of it at the press conference tomorrow. That may help reassure the public that the investigation is progressing."

∽

YVONNE CLOAKED herself with mac and scarf, grabbing her bag from the corner of the desk. She checked her watch. Nine-thirty. It had been a manic day. The rest of CID had already left.

Several cars sat in the station car park, most belonging to the late shift. Thankful she wasn't on late, she threw her bag onto the passenger seat and fired up the engine, unaware of another car being started on the opposite side of the car park.

She clicked on the music system, listening to an old Keane album she'd found in her bedroom drawer. The gentle strains of 'Bed shaped' struck up. Released the week he lay in a coma, it would always remind her of her late husband, David. She had listened to it, the morning he died.

She thought of him often. Still needing the occasional quiet time to grieve. This album represented that for her. It was cathartic. An album she loved and yet, one that hurt. Before she had even left town, salty rivers meandered down her cheeks, blurring the taillights in front of her. She wiped them away with the back of her hand, letting out a barely audible sob.

Full beams on, she left the town traffic behind and headed out onto the dark. She turned the music off.

A vehicle approached from behind. Gaining on her. She realised her speed had slowed to thirty miles an hour. She sped up to a respectable forty.

As they rounded a bend, he dazzled her with full beams.

"What the...?" She slowed down and pulled to the left, giving the other car room to overtake. It didn't. Instead, the driver honked and flashed his headlights.

A dirty number plate meant she couldn't make out the registration. An overwhelming feeling of dread welled inside her, her heart banging in her chest.

She pulled into a lay-by and extracted her warrant card, expecting the other driver to stop and have a go.

She needn't have worried, the other car sped on. Paying her no further heed. She placed a hand to her heart and bent forward, to slow her breathing and stop herself from being sick. It was a good ten minutes before she was ready to resume her journey.

7

LIGHTNING STRIKES

The sky was a uniform grey. The grey that is a fine drizzle. Slow and insidious. Penetrating clothing, hungry to find skin.

Yvonne had chosen a light coat and regretted that decision. A shiver travelled the length of her.

"Everything all right, ma'am?" Dewi leaned his head, studying her face.

Yvonne placed her hands deep in her pockets. "I think someone just walked over my grave." She gave a wry smile. "I'm fine. Thank you, Dewi. But not looking forward to this."

Dewi shook his head. "Me neither."

They walked uphill for around a quarter of a mile along a narrow lane, bisected along its length by a thin line of grass. The muddy, puddle-ridden track was, cordoned off. Yvonne almost fell into the hedge twice, trying to keep her balance on the designated, foot-wide strip.

At the top, on a wooded ridge above the village of Abermule, lay the ruins of Dolforwyn Castle. Built by Prince Llewellyn-Ap-Gruffydd, the last prince of Wales, the castle was difficult to reach, and not visible from the road. For tourists, it was a hidden gem.

The Severn Valley disappeared into the mist below. Yvonne shuddered, as they reached the blue-and-white police cordon.

Callum squeezed the tip of his cigarette out and came to greet them.

"What have we got?" She squinted, struggling to see through the mass of plastic-suited colleagues.

"Another set of remains." He rubbed the back of his neck. "The perp staged everything. Just like the last time. There's a knife pinned under the jaw of the victim and she's wearing a blood-stained dress."

The DI scanned the horizon. "Same signature, different method of killing."

Callum continued. "Someone cleaned the bones again. The photographer is still working up there. They have asked us to stay back until he's finished."

Yvonne nodded. "Is Hanson here?"

Callum pointed to a white tent. "Over there, talking to SOCO."

"Okay, good." Yvonne ran a hand through her damp hair. "I guess, we'll just have to wait."

"Shame we couldn't get a car up here." Dewi pulled a face.

Yvonne lifted the cordon. "Come on. We'll see if SOCO have spare suits."

∼

THE JAW BONE hung low as though the victim was still screaming. The DI suspected that was the intention. Several teeth were absent. Tangled, dark hair, clung to scraps of dried scalp. The perpetrator had tied this back in a rough ponytail using a red ribbon and placed it, like a cap, on the top of the skull. The torn dress had been navy blue and patterned with tiny white flowers. Many of the flowers were now a rusty brown, the victim having lost a lot of blood at the time of her death.

Yvonne's plastic suit crackled as she knelt next to the pathologist. "Was she an older victim?"

Hanson shook his head. "I don't think so. All the signs point to the victim being young."

"But, the teeth?"

"It looks like someone pulled them out, after she was already dead."

"To slow identification..."

"Most likely." Hanson signalled for the stretcher as he rose to his feet. "This victim was killed more recently."

"Fresh?" Yvonne's eyes widened.

"Not that recent. But, less than a year. We'll get the remains carbon dated. Give you a better idea."

"I'm amazed that you can estimate the time in the ground by looking at the bones."

Hanson smiled. "I can't. It was the smell and slime in the excavated grave." He pulled a face. "You get a nose for it."

"I see." Yvonne rose to her feet, rubbing her chin.

"This throws a spanner in the works." Dewi said, taking photographs with his mobile.

Yvonne nodded. "We focussed on Nicole Benoit's close associates, but it looks like we have a serial killer."

"Here we go again." Dewi sighed.

"I'm guessing, we don't knowing if sexual assaults occurred?" Yvonne asked Hanson.

The pathologist shook his head. "We didn't get useable DNA from the clothing of the last victim." He pointed to the current remains. "I doubt very much we'll get anything from her dress. We'll do a thorough search, as always, for hair and fibres and hope that throws up something."

"We need the identity of this girl, ASAP. If we can't identify her from dental records, we'll need Wyn Sealander to work his magic again." Yvonne walked over to where DC Jones chatted with SOCO. "Callum, can you check mis per records covering the last two years?"

"Will do, ma'am."

She returned to the pathologist. "Roger, was her throat was slit, as the set-up by the killer implies?"

"It's possible. Striations on the neck vertebrae suggest they took the knife right the way through to the bone. With the help of anthropology, I should be able to tell you whether someone attacked her from the front or from behind."

"Thank you, Roger."

"Oh, also, the photographer got three-dimensional images of two footprints."

"That's good news." Yvonne walked to the cordon and removed her plastic suits. "I have a bad feeling about this."

"Ma'am?" Dewi took her used suit and placed it in a pile with his.

"This victim was more recent. I hope I'm wrong, but this could be the buildup to something much bigger. This killer wants attention and will work his butt off to ensure he gets it. I mean, drilling every bone in a person's body, not once but twice, then threading all of them together with wire. We are talking days and days of constant toil." She looked Dewi in the eye. "We'll make sure he gets a lot more attention than he bargained for."

∽

THE DOOR OPENED, and she stumbled in surprise.

"Don't tell me. You need my help." Wyn grinned at her, once more barefoot, his shirt, open at the neck.

"How did you...?"

"I saw you from the window." He pointed to the pale-blue, Victorian frames with their imperfect glass. "I wasn't sure it was you, at first. I was staring at the view, with a mug of tea. I saw a car pull in and wondered who it was."

Yvonne smiled. "What would you have done if I had fallen flat on my face, when you opened the door?"

"Why, I'd have picked you up and dusted you down."

The DI cleared her throat. "We need your help. Someone left us another set of remains."

"Were the bones cleaned and strung together again?"

She nodded. "They're with the lab. The perp buried the body sometime within the last twelve months. Someone unearthed it, just like before."

"So, they killed this one *after* Nicole."

"Yes."

"And you'd like my help to reconstruct her face."

"I ought to say, she has missing teeth. We think the killer extracted them, after her death, to make identification more difficult."

Wyn sucked his top lip. "Hm... It makes shaping the mouth area tricky. Knowing whether the teeth were straight, sticking out, or going inwards, is a big help. It helps me to get the bite right. However, it shouldn't affect the overall likeness too much. I think we'll be okay."

"We'll have the skull with you as soon as we can."

Wyn hesitated.

"Is that all right?" Yvonne tilted her head.

"I'll be away a few days. I'll get on with it as soon as I'm back."

"No problem. That should fit in nicely."

"Since you're here, would you like a brew? The kettle's not long boiled."

She gazed out of the window at the rain pounding the road outside. "Do you know what? I'd like that. Thank you."

∽

"So, what made you become a police officer? Do you *like* working grisly murders?" Wyn handed her a steaming mug of tea and led her to a battered leather sofa at one end of the room.

"I didn't know what I wanted to do when I left school." Yvonne plumped down on the sofa. "And, if you'd told me I'd spend most my working career hunting serial killers, I think I'd have run a mile."

Wyn laughed. "So...?"

"I'm fascinated by mysteries and mysterious things. Not having an answer doesn't *feel* right. I *have* to know." She took a sip of tea before continuing. "I remember reading about Jack The Ripper, as a girl, and being frustrated that they never solved the case. That, and cases like Rachel Nickell, had me wondering if I could do something. If I could help the victims and their families."

"So, you became a police officer."

She stared into her tea. "A sudden, or violent, death is devastating for all involved. I became a police officer and told myself that I would work a case and never stop until I solved it." She sighed. "I have a vivid imagination. I see the victims in their last moments, crying out for help. I have a need to catch the killers and see them punished. We owe them that — the victims of crime. Someone believed they had the right to take away someone else's most treasured possession — their life. I can't bear for that to go unpunished. Wow, sorry." Yvonne grimaced. "Off on one."

"It's okay. It's a safe space." Wyn chuckled. "Besides, I'm interested."

"What about you?"

"Me?"

"What got you into reconstructing faces?"

Wyn shrugged. "I started out in fine art — painting, drawing, dabbling in photography. I always felt like something was missing. I couldn't put my finger on what that was. Then, much like yourself, I watched a documentary about facial reconstruction being used to resurrect dead people. Give them back their face, so to speak. Help identify them. Something went off in my head and I applied to Dundee University and got onto a course. I retrained and here I am, helping you." He continued. "A lot of my work comes from crime and I go where the money is. A guy's got to eat." He rubbed his chin. "Like you, I find it rewarding when my work helps solve cases. I give the victims life again."

The words 'playing God' flashed through Yvonne's mind. She didn't give voice to them. Instead, she gulped more of her tea and turned her gaze to the rain outside. "We're very thankful you retrained," she said.

They passed The next few minutes in a comfortable silence. Both finishing their tea whilst watching the rain and listening to it patter on the skylight.

When they had finished, the DI rose. "We'd better get back to work." She walked to the door. "I'll be in touch when you return."

Wyn smiled. "I'll look forward to it."

8

NO LET UP

Twenty-three-year-old, Sharon Sutton secured her bike to the railings near Harry Tuffin's petrol station, in Churchstoke, a small town on the Powys-Shropshire border.

She opened the panier and took out her purse, ready to buy a drink and sandwiches.

"Hello. Can you help me?"

A vehicle had pulled over on the road ahead. The driver was holding up a map and shrugging his shoulders, a confused look on his face.

She placed the purse in her shoulder bag and ran to the car. "Are you lost?"

He scratched his head, his cheeks reddening. "I think I am. I'm looking for this place." He put a finger on the map.

She couldn't see where he was pointing. "What's it called?"

"Er, I'm not sure how to pronounce it."

"Let me look." Sharon moved in closer as the driver opened the passenger door for her to better view the map.

"There..." He pointed again.

Sharon peered at where his finger tapped the paper. It was the middle of nowhere.

Her breath caught in her throat as he pulled her headlong into the vehicle and rubbed something noxious in her face with a cloth.

Everything became a blur, and she passed out.

∾

He sniffed the acrid air, allowing it to tease the hair in his nostrils until he sneezed. The smell of burning irritated the membranes of his nose as the bit drilled into the bone held by the clamp and stand. He lifted his hinged, close-work lenses and blew at the hole, flicking the lenses back in place to examine the tiny corridor. The fruits of his labour.

He released the bone from the clamp, replacing it with another, all the while humming 'Yellow' by Coldplay, the tune off-key, licking the film of vaporised material from his lips, as he recommenced drilling.

Below him, on the polythene-covered floor, the rest of the remains. Cleaned-up bones positioned as in life. The essence of the woman.

Several days he had applied himself. And, now laid out in all its glory, the prepped scaffolding ready to take the wire which would once more articulate it.

He grabbed the roll, unwinding just enough before snipping it with cutters. He resisted licking the end before threading it through the pre-made holes and winding it together to finish the connection.

In a far corner of the room, a metal bin contained the cooked-off flesh. Pig food. It stank. He didn't like it. Later that night he would get rid.

∼

"SHALL WE DANCE?"

The bones clacked together as he grabbed both wrists and hoisted them. He whirled his macabre partner round the room, polythene crackling beneath his feet, his hands sweaty inside latex gloves. The humming, louder and more off-key. His glazed eyes wide and unblinking. The skull of his dance partner, angled backwards. Her bones clacking time with the music in his head.

He continued for several minutes in this fantasy. A room full of people. Admirers of a couple at one and in motion. All staring at them. Wanting to be them.

He whirled her around, her backbone against his torso, his voice taking on a menacing growl. "You're stepping on my toes? Why are you stepping on my toes?" He twisted one wrist behind her back with his right hand, whilst he rammed his left forearm into her throat. "You watching him? Is that it? I'm not good enough? I'm never good enough for you."

He turned her back around to face him, his gloved hand gripping her lower jaw. "Don't think I don't know what you're imagining. Don't think I don't know you've been there in your head."

∼

YVONNE COULDN'T BELIEVE what she'd heard. A tight knot developed in her stomach. Her worst fears, realised.

Dewi put an arm out to block her from seeing the remains. He shook his head. The colour had disappeared from his face. "It's not pleasant, ma'am."

She nudged his arm aside. "Murder never is, Dewi."

"But, this-"

"Please, Dewi. I want to see for myself. Anyway, I want to speak to Tozer."

"He's over there, next to the body."

She donned plastic suit and overshoes and made her way through to where Will Tozer and the SOCO personnel were working.

"We meet again." Tozer's looked pale, as though he was about to throw up.

In front of Yvonne, the victim sat propped against one of the standing stones of Mitchell's Fold Stone Circle - a Bronze Age monument, on Stapeley Hill, with views far into the distance, in every direction.

Will stood at her shoulder. "It looks like someone strangled this one. Broken hyoid bone. It's the same signature. Bones stripped, drilled, and pieced back together again with wire."

"Is the pathologist here?"

Tozer nodded. "He's over there." He touched her arm. "Don't go there."

"Why?"

"Her flesh is..." He grimaced. "The killer removed it from the bones and left it in a heap next to them."

Yvonne shook her head. Words failed.

Tozer toe-poked the ground in front of him. "He's becoming more confident."

The DI nodded. "A different MO. A girl killed and processed, not buried and excavated. This is not a good development."

"It's a nightmare. The clothing is covered in blood." He pointed. "That's the rest of her, there."

Yvonne walked over to the pile of flesh, tossed in a heap. Her torso convulsed. She turned and threw up her entire stomach contents. "Oh, God. Sorry. Sorry." She wiped her mouth with the back of her gloved hand, her face drawn.

"It won't take long to discover who she was." Will

pointed to the bright yellow t-shirt with the smiley-face logo and jeans, in which the perp had clad the skeleton.

Dewi was back at her side. "Callum and Dai think they have come up with a likely candidate." He checked his notes. "A missing woman, twenty-three years old, name of Sharon Sutton. She vanished ten days ago."

"Sharon Sutton." Yvonne knelt by the remains. "So young..." She rose to her feet, turning around and scanning the trees. "Okay, you bastard, you got our attention. You can stop with the killing."

She turned to Deli, gritting her teeth. "I want the exact circumstances of her disappearance, ASAP. Where she was, who she was with. Everything you can get."

"Will do, ma'am."

Hanson pointed to the jaw. "The killer removed none of this victim's teeth."

Yvonne clenched her fists. "He didn't need to. He wanted her identified." She switched to Hanson. "Can you get us details of the tools used, so we can compare?"

Hanson nodded. "We'll need a week."

"Good. Let's be sure we're not dealing with a copycat killer." She turned back to Dewi. "You said she could be Sharon Sutton?"

"That's right."

"Request dental records and invite friends and relatives to speak with us."

"On it, ma'am."

"Can you tell the team, there's an urgent briefing this afternoon. Inform the DCI."

Dewi put up his hand in acknowledgement as he turned to leave the field.

∽

Callum and Dai filled Yvonne in, ahead of the briefing.

"Everything we know about Sharon's disappearance fits." Callum ran a hand across his brow. "The timeframe is right. The clothing is right."

Dai checked his notes. "We've retrieved Sharon's bicycle from outside Harry Tuffin's garage, in Churchstoke and requested their CCTV. A witness describes Sharon securing her bike to the lamppost outside, but they didn't continue watching after that. So, they don't know what happened next."

Callum grunted. "The two members of staff working at the garage that day, don't recall seeing Sharon."

Yvonne pursed her lips. "Perhaps, she didn't get as far as going inside. I mean, wearing that distinctive yellow t-shirt, she would have stood out."

"I agree." Dai nodded.

"As soon as we get the CCTV footage, I'd like to see it. Okay? Make sure we get everything they have. If they have other cameras, I want the footage from them, too. I want everything recorded on the day she disappeared."

9

THE PATHOLOGIST

The briefing was a subdued affair.

Yvonne looked at the DCI, at the skin sagging under his eyes. She felt for him. He had fielded a ridiculous number of calls, and attempts to interview them, by local and national press. Several times, they'd invaded his front garden and even now, journalists followed him to and from work. It seemed like the entire world had an interest in their maniac and it didn't the patience to wait for answers.

The rest of the team talked in low voices, their nervous excitement palpable by the level of fidgeting and sighs.

Wyn Sealander was the last to join them. Due to talk about his work and unveil photographs, he waited at the back while the DI ran through known details.

"Okay, everyone. I'll get straight on with it. We've had the DNA results for the remains found at Mitchell's fold Stone Circle. They *are* those of twenty-three-year-old Sharon Sutton. Dewi and I will talk to her parents and try to fill in the gaps regarding her movements, especially those leading up to her disappearance. This afternoon, we will also view the CCTV from the garage where she left her bike, while uniform carry out door-to-door enquiries with Churchstoke residents."

She continued. "Dewi and Callum, I'd like you to help me go through the footage. I'd like the rest of the team to interview any witnesses, identified by the door-to-door enquiries. Did she go with her killer? Or, was she abducted? If we can get the answer to that, it will help identify the methods used by our killer to choose his victims. This latest killing signals an escalation by the perpetrator and makes our job much more urgent. We are no longer dealing with cold cases. The killer may already have chosen his next victim."

She pointed at the anthropologist. "I will hand you over to Wyn Sealander, who is reconstructing the second victim's face. Thank you."

Wyn cleared his throat as he left his seat. "Thank you, Yvonne and thanks for inviting me to give this talk."

Dai helped Wyn to connect his lap top to the projector for the white board. "I'll print hard copies out for all of you, later."

He fiddled with the laptop until satisfied with the display. "This where I'm at with the second victim."

Yvonne stared at the image. "It's really coming along," she murmured.

Wyn's talk on reconstruction drew a lot of praise. His sympathetic rendering of the first victim, showed such attention to detail. It could have been a photograph.

"This has to be finished within the next couple of days. It goes to the nation at six o'clock on Wednesday. It should be on the internet early Wednesday afternoon."

Wyn used a laser pen to direct their attention to photographs of the second victim's remains, as they were found. "The victim had long, dark hair. The killer tied the remaining hair in a ponytail, using a bow. I am reproducing this in my reconstruction. I'm assuming the killer dresses his victims in their real clothing and in the way they were dressed when he abducted them."

He flicked to the next slide. "The killer could alter certain features so, for the sake of completeness, I will produce photographs with the hair worn down over the shoulders. He gazed at the screen. I hope that when I finish, someone will know who she is. Any questions?"

The noise level rose as officers discussed the images.

"What were the results from SOCO? Were the victims raped?" DCI Llewellyn directed his question at Yvonne.

"We have no way of knowing, sir. The perp cooked the flesh off the latest victim. That eradicated any traces of semen. And the cold case victims..." She sighed. "We don't anything other than bones and clothing. What I can tell you, is the clothing contained no trace other than blood from the victim. They are doing a meticulous check for fibres. Nothing found, so far."

Llewellyn rubbed his chin, his movements slow. "Thank you, Yvonne."

∼

AFTER THE BRIEFING, Yvonne sat checking her scribbled notes, underlining the need to talk to Sharon Sutton's parents.

Her thoughts turned to the DCI. Though under pressure, he had pushed none onto her. She admired his strength and his sense of responsibility. She decided to go and speak to him.

Wyn came to see her before she had the chance.

She smiled. "That was impressive." She meant it.

"Thank you, Yvonne." He smiled back. "Amazing enough for me to have dinner with the lead detective?"

"Sorry?"

"With you... Does my great work qualify me to take you out tomorrow night? Dinner?"

She frowned. "Wyn, I-"

"I'm buying. You look like you need a break. One night."

She looked up at him. His wavy hair, staying only just the right side of tame. This, and his open-neck, collarless shirt and sandals, gave him a bohemian air. The air of freedom.

She grinned. "Since you asked so nicely, yes. I would like that. I would like it very much."

"Great. I'll look forward to it, Yvonne." Wyn's eyes sparkled, his lips seemed to linger her name.

∼

Pensive, Yvonne turned to watch him leave and caught sight of the DCI in the doorway. She saw something in those tired eyes. It looked like disappointment. He disappeared with the crime commissioner. Her chance had passed. She returned to her notes, feeling awkward.

∼

"There you go." Dewi plopped a mug of tea onto her desk. "You look like you need a cuppa."

"Oh, thank you, Dewi." She reached for it. "You read my thoughts."

Callum threw his jacket onto the back of his chair and forwarded the CCTV footage to the relevant timestamp.

The DI and Dewi watched the screen as Callum talked them through it.

"This is where it starts. We've scrutinised the footage and there are no other sightings of Sharon before this point."

"What time is that?" Yvonne squinted.

"3.20 pm."

"Did you check whether that was accurate?"

"We've checked, ma'am, and it is within five seconds."

"Okay, good."

"She comes into frame here, riding her bike. She brakes, dismounts and reaches into her panier for the bike lock. You can't make out her expression, but her body language suggests she's relaxed."

"Okay, bike secured by...," Yvonne leaned towards the screen, "three-twenty-four pm."

"Right." Callum nodded. "She approaches Harry Tuffin's garage, but appears to change her mind and walks in the opposite direction. A few steps, and we lose her." Callum pulled a face. "Not a single camera caught her after that point. The cameras are on the garage forecourt and the road outside. The next camera is some distance away, and she appears nowhere on it."

"Wait. Rewind. Let's watch that again."

Callum did as directed.

"There. She's reacting to someone. It's a shame we can't see her face. Rewind again."

Callum rewound once more.

"Can you slow it?"

"There you go."

Yvonne pursed her lips. "She's talking to someone. Someone on the road."

"I agree. She's saying something." Dewi rubbed his chin. "Whoever she's talking to is just out of view."

Yvonne sighed. "Frustrating. They stayed back from the camera."

"She was likely abducted in a vehicle." Dewi drank a gulp of his tea. "We should check out all vehicles, passing nearby cameras, within the relevant timeframe. Cross-check them against vehicles of known offenders."

"We thought of that. Dai is on the case." Callum tapped his pen on the desk.

"What about the garage? Did she go in at any point?" Yvonne asked.

Callum shook his head. "The CCTV supports what the staff have been saying. We examined the complete footage from the shop and she is nowhere on it."

Yvonne finished her tea. "It's even more important they carry out thorough door-to-door enquiries near that garage. I'll speak to Will Tozer and see if West Mercia have found any witnesses around Priest Weston. Tourist season is just hotting up. Maybe they'll strike *lucky*."

"Let's hope SOCO have something. Fibres would be nice." Dewi rose from his seat.

Yvonne nodded. "I'll tell Tozer what we saw on the footage."

10

PRESSURE

Yvonne rang the bell of the whitewashed, semi-detached home of Clive and Debbie Sutton. There was no answer, but they could hear people inside. Dewi paced and Yvonne played with her bottom lip.

When forty-nine-year-old Clive Sutton opened the door to them, he did so whilst fighting with an unopened suitcase in the hallway. His greying hair stuck out in various directions

"Bloody thing." His mouth contorted in that painful way it does when your whole body is screaming but no sound emanates. Tears dropped off both sides of his chin.

"Mr Sutton? We're detectives from Dyfed Powys police. I'm Yvonne Giles and this is Dewi Hughes. May we come in?"

He moved back, almost toppling over the suitcase. Behind him, were yet more suitcases and a large pile of washing.

"We got back from Tuscany after she went missing. Got the first available flight." His eyes were large and unfocussed. "I don't know what to do with myself."

Yvonne placed a gentle hand on his arm. "Shall we sit?"

Dewi lined the suitcases up along the wall.

"My wife's in here..." He led them through to a small sitting room. The news was on with the volume turned down.

Clive pointed to it. "We've been watching for any developments."

Yvonne frowned. "Have victim liaison officers been to see you?"

He nodded. "We sent them away. My wife wasn't ready. The shock..."

"It must have been hard. I can imagine." Yvonne's eyes were soft. "Just so long as you're aware they are there to help."

She turned her gaze to Debbie, who was staring into space, clasping a photograph of her dead daughter in one hand and a mug of something she wasn't drinking in the other. Her skin, as pale as the walls. Her eyes, sunken and red.

She turned to the detectives. "They made a mistake. It happens sometimes. They don't know it's Sharon. How can they? They only found bones. It's not Sharon. She's with her friends." Debbie turned her gaze away.

"I'll make a brew." Dewi left for the kitchen.

Clive turned to Yvonne. "How sure *are* they?"

Yvonne tilted her head, her lips a thin line. "Very. They used dental records. I'm so sorry, Mr Sutton."

Clive shook his head. "She was staying with friends at their flat. They called us to say she hadn't come home. We thought she might have been here. We rang and rang this number." Clive put his head in his hands. "I knew something was wrong. She wasn't one to let anyone down. She wouldn't have left her friends wondering where she was."

"Your daughter lived with you?"

"Since last Christmas. She broke up with her boyfriend and moved back in with us." Saliva dripped from his lips. He appeared not to notice. "Who would do this? She had everything to live for."

Debbie Sutton let out a heart-wrenching howl. The photograph fell to the floor.

Yvonne knelt to retrieve it. She placed it on the sofa next to Debbie. "I'm sorry to ask this. Was Sharon seeing anyone else?"

Clive shook his head.

"What about her ex-boyfriend? Had she had any contact with him?"

"Not since February, when they split. She said they were still on friendly terms. They were childhood sweethearts, but they'd grown apart. Wanted different things. I saw him with someone else. Sharon didn't seem to mind one bit. She carried on smiling and having fun, like she always did."

"Did she talk of meeting anyone else?"

"We asked Dave and Carol that question." He scratched his head. "They're the friends she stays with. They said she was going for a bike ride by herself. She often did that. She told them she would grab something to eat while she was out. They were sure she hadn't mentioned meeting anyone."

"Why was she staying with friends? Why didn't she stay here?"

"She didn't like staying anywhere on her own. Even here, at night. Ever since she was little. Used to sleep walk as a child. She suffered with night terrors."

"I see."

Dewi returned with a tray of mugs and a full teapot.

Clive sighed. "Thank you. We haven't been eating or drinking much since..."

Yvonne's hands clenched into fists. "We will do everything we can to catch your daughter's killer. Whatever it takes."

Clive looked at her, his eyes studying her face. "I believe you."

∽

"Seems we have a name for our killer." Callum, scratched at his stubble and tossed several newspapers onto Yvonne's desk.

'Who is The Pathologist?' screamed one headline. 'Pathologist who solves his own crimes' screamed another, with a subheading: 'And he's better at it than the police.'

"That's great. Just great." Yvonne pulled a face, leaning back with her arms folded across her chest.

"Hacks, ma'am." Callum laughed at her serious expression. "You know the score. They wouldn't sell many papers with headlines suggesting the investigation was ticking along nicely, now, would they?"

"Has the DCI seen these?"

"Not yet. Well, unless he's bought his own." Callum placed his hands in his trouser pockets. "Do you want me to show him?"

"No." She said. "He looks exhausted. Those *hacks* are hounding him. I feel bad we don't have more than we do."

"Do you think he's familiar with police procedure?"

"Who, the DCI?" She raised an eyebrow at her DC.

"No." Callum laughed. "The killer."

Yvonne shrugged. "Who isn't familiar with police work? There are CSI programmes on every channel, these days. Plus, you can find anything you want on the internet. We have Tasha's profile. I'll speak to her about the latest find and see if that helps her refine it. Either way, it's almost certain that these are stranger murders. When we catch him, it'll be because he's slipped up and left forensic traces or got caught on CCTV. What's worrying me, is that he's probably hunting future victims. That's something we must stop. I'll speak to the DCI about going public with the profile. We need a name and fast."

~

WYN WAS WAITING, leaning his back against the restaurant facade, as her taxi arrived at La Terraza Italian restaurant fifteen minutes late.

"I'm sorry, I-"

He held up his hand. "It's okay. No need to apologise. I only just got here myself."

She took in his dark suit and tie and regretted her decision not to wear the navy-blue maxi dress. It lay in a crumpled heap on her bed, with a variety of other tried-ons and could-have-beens. A horror lying in wait for her return.

Clothed in a white cotton blouse and cropped trousers, she eyed Wyn's tie and chewed her lip. He didn't look himself. "You're smart." It sounded like an accusation.

He chuckled. "You cannot imagine how many potential outfits I went through, trying to guess what you might wear."

"Oh, I do. I really do." She joined him in laughter, feeling relieved.

As their garrulous, Italian host seated them in a corner, the recent tension eased from her.

They chose a bottle of the house red. A full-bodied chianti. They drank their first glass while choosing from the menu.

"Whoa." She put a hand over her glass.

Wyn stopped pouring her a second helping. "What's the matter?"

"I've eaten barely a thing, today."

"And?" Wyn raised an eyebrow.

Yvonne giggled. "It's been a while since I was drunk. It's not pretty."

Wyn loosened his tie and winked at her, giving her a boyish smile. "Who cares?"

She took her hand away. "Did you find it hard?"

"What?"

"Entering college for a second time... Starting over again?"

"Not as hard as you might think." Wyn rubbed his cheek. "I mean, money was tight. I'd earned peanuts as a fine artist and was living cheek-by-jowl on a tiny loan. The learning wasn't hard. I came alive. It invigorated me. I was gaining a needed skill and enjoying it. Besides, when I graduated, I expected to earn a decent wage."

"Couldn't you do that with fine art?"

Wyn thought about it. "You can, but it's not guaranteed. Commissions are irregular. Some people get lucky. I didn't." He finished his glass and poured another as the starters arrived.

Yvonne eyed her ravioli with relish.

"What about you? Were you always a detective?"

She shook her head. "I started out in science. My degree was in microbiology. I met my husband at university."

Wyn frowned. "Husband?"

She sighed. "My *late* husband David."

"Oh, I *am* sorry."

"It's okay." She took a gulp of chianti. "It was several years ago. I miss him but, I try not to dwell..."

"What sort of man was he?" Enlarged pupils made the anthropologist's eyes appear black.

Yvonne's own took on a thousand-yard stare; her smile, wistful. "He loved flying, he loved metal, and he loved me."

"What happened? If you don't mind me asking?"

"An accident... on the airfield."

"Were you there when it happened?"

She nodded. "It was horrific. I still see it in nightmares, the accident and the aftermath."

"I'm sorry, I don't mean to bring you down."

"My friend, Tasha, helped a lot."

"The lady I met the other-"

"We met on my first serial murder case. She's a great character and a great friend." Yvonne ate some of her food.

"She seems a practical sort." His eyes held hers.

"She is. She gets stuck in and she always helps to clarify my thoughts."

"A fine friend to have."

"Yes."

"This is good." Wyn savoured a mouthful of his mushrooms, studying her face. "So, like me, you retrained so you could follow your passion?"

She nodded. "I did. And I haven't looked back. Though some cases tug at the heartstrings."

"I'll bet." Wyn paused between mouthfuls. "Like the current one."

She nodded.

"More chianti?" Wyn refilled her glass a further time.

"Why not?" She pushed her empty starter plate away. "In for a penny..."

Their main courses arrived, carbonara for Yvonne and stuffed aubergine for Wyn.

Yvonne smiled.

"What?"

"You, in a suit and tie."

"My dear lady, I can wear a suit and tie." He exaggerated a pained expression, putting a hand to his heart.

"I think I prefer you barefoot." She met his eyes before returning her to her food.

～

LIGHTHEADED, she stumbled on the restaurant steps, almost falling into the street.

Wyn caught her. "Are you all right?"

"Yes, thank you." She straightened, brushing herself down.

"I think I may have topped up our glasses a little too often. I'm a bit tipsy, myself."

"Our taxis will be here any minute." Yvonne yawned.

"Thank you for being such wonderful company." Wyn bent his head to peck her on the lips.

A moment later, she tasted the red wine on his, as the kiss deepened.

She pulled away. "I'm sorry, I-"

Wyn held up a hand. "No. *I'm* sorry. It was my fault."

"I'm not looking for anything. I'm not ready."

"Don't sweat it." Wyn pointed up the street. "Your taxi."

～

YVONNE KNOCKED on the DCI's door before pushing it open. "Is now okay?" she asked the top of his head.

He paused writing and checked his watch. "Sorry, I forgot to come see you. Can you forgive me? So much going on." He looked up at her, his desk awash with paper.

"No problem, sir. I guessed you were busy. I have several appointments this afternoon, however, and-"

"How was the meal?" He took off his reading glasses and placed them on his desk.

"Last night? Good. Food... nice. Thank you." She coloured, clearing her throat.

"Did Wyn behave like a gentleman?"

"He did."

"And you? Did you behave like a lady?" He grinned but there was something serious lurking in his eyes.

"Always." She forced a laugh.

His gaze lingered on her face. "Right. Well, we should discuss the latest developments in the case. I'm under a lot of pressure. I know you're doing the best you can but, this latest development..."

She nodded, fighting the lump in her throat. "Women are panicking and I can't say I blame them."

"What leads do you have?"

She put a hand to her brow. "I'm still following up associates of the girls. But, I suspect we are dealing with a stranger to all of them. A serial killer. What we don't know, is whether we're hunting an opportunist or a stalker. We're working on that. He's careful not to leave trace evidence." She sucked her upper lip. "I have a strong feeling he's stalking the women for some time, before taking them."

"What makes you say that?"

"He kidnapped Sharon Sutton close to a major garage, but avoided every single CCTV camera. According to the shop assistants, Sharon regularly visited that garage on her bike rides. He only had to watch and wait. Easy-peasy." Yvonne scratched her head and continued. "I think he ambushed Nicole Benoit on the Long Mynd. They found her bicycle near the upper carpark. The place is a busy tourist spot and yet he killed and buried her, without being seen. My gut tells me he plans these kills for some time."

The DCI nodded. "Well, it would fit with your psychologist friend's assessment..."

"It would."

"Yvonne. I hate to put pressure on you." He sighed. "However, I need something more concrete, ASAP."

Yvonne looked at him, her eyes unblinking. "I understand. We'll do everything we can to get it. I've got a great team. This won't defeat us for long."

"BBC Wales will be here tomorrow to film Wyn's reconstruction of the second victim."

She nodded. "We'll be ready."

∼

"A LITTLE DELICATE, ARE WE?" Dewi grinned at her, his eyes twinkling.

"Yeah. Hilarious, Dewi." She scowled at him. "I'd like to see you try holding it together with the DCI, when you're sick as a dog. I think twenty people invaded my head for a rave party."

"That bad?"

"Yes."

"You look pale." Dewi chuckled. "Here take some of this. It'll do you good." He handed her a coffee mug.

"Thanks. Sorry. I've been a right old grouch this morning. I'll be better when my head has cleared."

"You shouldn't be a dirty stop out," he said, winking at her.

She poked her tongue out. "How's the grandkids, anyway?"

"Good, but manic. Into everything and still needing their

bottoms wiped far too often. I can't complain, though. They're only little once. George starts big school next month."

"Gosh, that's flown by."

"Tell me about it." Dewi shook his head. "Anyway, what did the DCI say?"

"He wants us to get a move on with this case. Not that he needs to ask. We do this for the victims." She put a hand to her forehead. "Wyn should have a reconstruction of the Dolforwyn victim for us later today. It'll be on national TV by tomorrow night. Finger's crossed we get an identity soon."

11

KATIE DENHAM

Yvonne knocked on the door of Wyn's studio and waited for him to cease work and let her in. She waited almost a minute and was about to leave.

A wavy-haired head appeared inch-by-inch around the door.

"Have I come at a bad time?" She grimaced, stepping back.

"No. No, not at all." He opened the door wider. "You've picked a good time, actually. I have something for you."

She cast her eyes around the room, and to the centre of the main workbench. "You've finished."

"Meet the girl from Dolforwyn." He bowed exaggeratedly. "I hope you approve."

"Wow." Yvonne crossed over to examine the likeness. "She's beautiful, just like the first victim." She took in the high cheekbones, blonde hair, and fine features. "You've done an amazing job, Wyn. She's looking at me as though she knows things. Things, I don't." The DI pursed her lips.

Wyn tilted his head to one side. "Well, that's true. I mean, she knows the identity of her killer and…"

"I don't. Thanks for reminding me."

"I didn't mean-"

She held a hand up. "Don't sweat it. It's true."

"The hairstyle is an approximation." He scratched his chin, the lines deepening on his forehead. "I've put it in a bun, but I've photographed it both up and down. The hair they found was a matted mess. The ribbon in it suggests she wore it up."

"Someone will recognise her from this, Wyn, I'm sure. You've excelled yourself again."

"Thank you. You know, I thought you were avoiding me." Wyn took a step closer to her.

"Avoiding? Oh, no. I've been busy the last couple of days. Our DCI is desperate for a breakthrough. His patience is wearing thin and I can't say I blame him. BBC Wales are coming to film your work tomorrow afternoon. Are you ready?"

"Sure am." He cast his eyes around his studio.

"It's okay. They won't be looking at any mess." She smiled. "Just your artistry."

"Can I see you later?" he asked, looking at his bare feet. He wiggled his toes. "See? I'm prepared."

She laughed. "Oh, you remember what I said when I'd had a few."

"Totally." He pouted, holding his palms up, as though asking how she could doubt him.

She thought about the DCI and the press conference the following day. "I'd better not, Wyn. Sorry to let you down, but we have an early start tomorrow and I need to have my thoughts straight."

"Does that mean I get your thoughts all muddled up?" He winked at her.

She cleared her throat. "Not at all." Her smile suggested, 'maybe'.

∼

"We've got a name." Dewi fast-paced to her desk. "A Susan Denham has been in touch to say she believes the Dolforwyn Castle victim is her daughter, Katie Denham." Dewi checked his notes. "Disappeared a year ago, aged nineteen."

"Where from?"

"Welshpool, ma'am." He handed her his notebook.

"How soon can we get confirmation that she *is* Katie?"

"They've taken Blood samples from mum for DNA analysis. In the meantime, she handed in these." He tossed several photographs onto the DI's desk.

Yvonne flicked through. "This one. That's the-"

"The yellow smiley-face t-shirt she was wearing the day she went missing."

"All right, Dewi. This is great, but we can't go public until we get the DNA results. Please tell Mrs Denham that we'll be in touch as soon as we are sure. Tell her I would like to speak to her, anyway."

"Ma'am?"

"Even if our victim is not her daughter, we should still investigate Katie's disappearance. It could be related. I'm surprised this case wasn't higher on police radar already."

"I think it would have been if Katie hadn't had a history of disappearing."

"Running away?"

"Twice, according to Mrs Denham. Her daughter liked her independence. She spent two months back-packing around Europe with friends, before she disappeared. She hadn't told her family she was going."

Yvonne frowned. "How do you know all this?"

Dewi grinned. "I read the file."

"Okay. Well, inform me the minute those DNA results come back."

"Will do, ma'am."

∽

"Thank you for agreeing to talk, Mrs Denham."

"You can call me Susan." Mrs Denham stood back to allow the detective into her hallway.

Yvonne cast a quick glance over everything. She pointed to the photographs on the wall of the hallway. Vibrant photographs, framed in black. "Your daughter was a beautiful and lively girl, Susan. I am so sorry for your loss."

"Come into the sitting room." Susan led her through a doorway and pointed to a suede couch. "Please, take a seat."

Yvonne took out her notebook, one eye taking in the porcelain cat collection on the sideboard.

Small in stature, Susan's hunched shoulders made her look smaller still. Her fading hair, only just tamed by the loose band attempting a ponytail.

"She was a free spirit. The number of times I warned her that she needed to take care and that the world could be a dangerous place. She said I was a smother mother. I expect she got that phrase from the kids in school."

"Teenage tantrums?"

"She never forgave me for upping sticks."

"You moved?"

Susan Denham nodded. "Until she was seventeen, we lived in Church Stretton. She was in school there."

Yvonne stared at her. "Church Stretton School?"

"Yes. Her father and I split up. I moved away. Katie came with me. But, she had wanted to stay put..."

Yvonne tilted her head. "She wanted to remain with her father?"

"No, not that. Katie preferred to live with me. She wanted to stay in Church Stretton." Susan stared at her shoes. "Thought she was in love with one of her teachers. She was doing 'A' levels and her work was suffering. I thought it healthier for us both to move. That's when we came to Welshpool."

Yvonne stared at her. "Which teacher?"

"Sorry?"

"Who was the teacher? Can you remember?"

"Oh, um... May... Mayton..."

"Maynard?"

"Yes, Maynard. She always referred to him as Craig. It was Craig Maynard. His wife helped run a riding stables. Katie had had lessons there."

"Do you mean Rosie?" Yvonne edged forward in her seat, leaning in towards Susan.

"I don't recall the woman's name. Could have been Rosie. Katie hadn't had many lessons before we moved. She had a few more at a local stables but decided that riding wasn't for her. She preferred her own two feet."

"Did she get on with Rosie?"

"She didn't say."

"What happened after you moved here?"

"She completed her 'A' levels at Welshpool High and then took off for three months back-packing around Europe. Didn't tell me where she was until weeks after she'd left. It worried me sick. I had hoped she might go to college, but she said she didn't want student debt hanging over her."

"Was she trying to find herself?" Yvonne asked, her voice soft.

"Yes, I guess she was."

"What happened when she disappeared? I checked the police files, and it seems we didn't categorise it as a 'missing and at risk' case."

"That was my fault." Susan sighed. "They asked me if she'd run away before. I said yes and admitted she may have gone travelling again. Katie had taken her purse, coat and mobile in a small rucksack. She'd talked about another walking tour on the continent. I thought she might have done that."

"But, you didn't hear from her."

"I was getting more concerned. I spoke to her father several times. He hadn't heard from her. I contacted missing persons charities and they could find no trace. They said people sometimes just want to disappear. I blamed myself. I felt guilty about moving her to Welshpool."

"Don't blame yourself. You couldn't have known."

"I still don't believe she's gone." Tears welled in Susan's eyes.

"I'm sorry to ask you a further question, but did you ever contact Church Stretton School or the teacher, Craig Maynard? Find out if she had contacted them? It might help to know where she was when she disappeared."

"I contacted the school. They said they'd had no contact from her. The day she left, she told me she was going hiking along the Kerry Ridgeway. She wasn't sure whether she'd be back that night. She gave me a kiss and told me she loved me. I told her to be careful. I didn't see her again."

"Was she going with someone?"

"As far as I know, she was going alone."

Tears ran down Susan Denham's cheeks.

"I'm so sorry." Yvonne put an arm around the other woman's shoulder. "Can I get you anything? Victim liaison officers will be back soon. Would you like me to call anyone else?"

Susan shook her head. "I want to be alone for a bit. I hope you understand."

Yvonne nodded. She was having her own battle with tears.

As she left, the DI set her face against the wind, more determined than ever to catch the devil behind the deaths.

12

COMMON DENOMINATOR

Raised voices and the sound of something smashing against a wall greeted Yvonne and Dewi, on their arrival at Craig and Rosie's place.

"Domestic?" Yvonne ran down the garden and banged on the door, pursued by her DS.

Dewi put his ear to it. "Sounds like they're arguing."

It was several minutes before Craig appeared. He tucked a flap of shirt back into his trousers.

"Police. We'd like to talk to you." Dewi announced.

"I know what this looks like." Craig ran a hand through his hair and stepped back to allow them to enter.

"We heard smashing crockery. Is anybody hurt?" Yvonne asked, as Rosie appeared in the kitchen doorway.

Craig shook his head. "Just an argument. We're both okay."

Yvonne pursed her lips. "We want to ask you a few questions. Will that be all right?"

Craig nodded. "Sure." His hand shook as he closed the front door behind them.

"Under the circumstances, I think it best if we speak to you in separate rooms." Yvonne walked towards Rosie. "Is that okay?"

Rosie turned back into the kitchen.

Craig led Dewi into the lounge.

∼

"WHAT WAS THAT ABOUT?" Dewi asked. He closed the lounge door.

"This and that. Everything. We're always arguing."

"Over what?"

"She says I'm irritating."

"For doing what?"

"Breathing?" Craig sighed.

"Who smashed the mug?"

Craig shook his head.

"You can get help. Have you ever considered counselling?"

"Did somebody call you? A neighbour?" Craig spat the words.

"No." Dewi took out his notebook. "We came here to ask you about a girl you used to teach. A girl called Katie. Katie Denham."

Craig frowned. "Katie Denham? I don't understand. You're the officers investigating the death of Nicole Benoit-"

"That's right."

"How is that related to Katie Denham?"

"Did you see the news this morning?"

Craig shook his head. "Why? What's happened?"

"We confirmed the identity of remains left at a local landmark."

Craig's mouth fell open, his eyes wide.

"I understand you taught Katie. We're contacting those who knew her. Those who could shed light on her last movements."

"Are you asking *all* her former teachers? I don't understand. Katie left our school years ago. Her schooling carried on elsewhere."

"That's right." Dewi nodded.

"Then, why?"

"Mrs Denham said Katie had a crush on you. We wondered if she might have contacted you before disappearing?"

"Wait, what do you mean disappearing? You mean she went missing? Like Nicole?"

"She did. They thought it possible she'd gone travelling, without telling her mum."

"When was that? When did she leave?" Craig frowned.

"Last summer."

"Last summer..." He rubbed his chin, eyes half-closed. "No. She didn't contact me."

"What about your wife? As I understand it, she used to attend your wife's riding school."

"She didn't speak to Rosie, as far as I am aware. She'd had riding lessons with Rosie, before she and her mother moved away from Church Stretton. I'm not aware of her having any more after they left."

"You're sure of that?"

"Yes."

~

"What happened?" Yvonne's eyes wandered over the shards

of mug scattered on the floor, its contents streaked down the kitchen wall.

"I was angry." Rosie coloured.

"Why?"

"He's never here." She exhaled with a loud puff. "Once upon a time, I couldn't get him from under my feet. A regular home-bird. Now? He's never in."

"Would it help to talk to someone? The two of you? Or, just you? There are excellent counselling services available. We could send you details."

"We won't last much longer." Rosie sighed. "As for counselling? We don't have the will."

"It might save your marriage." Yvonne tilted her head, trying to make contact with Rosie's downcast eyes.

"That's the point."

"We didn't come here about your argument." Yvonne pulled a chair out from under the kitchen table. "Do you mind?"

"Help yourself." Rosie grabbed another. "I could do with sitting down."

"Do you remember a girl called Katie Denham?" Yvonne took out her pocketbook.

"Katie Denham?" Rosie wrinkled her nose in concentration. "Katie... Katie... Wait, is she the girl who moved to Welshpool? Blonde girl. Tall."

"That's the one." Yvonne handed her a photograph. "I understand she had lessons at your riding school. She left Church Stretton three years ago when her parents separated."

"What has that to do with us? Wait, he wasn't... Was he?"

Yvonne held up a hand. "Not that we are aware. We are talking to all her associates. We want to establish her movements before she disappeared."

"She disappeared?"

Yvonne nodded. "Someone murdered her. We found the remains and believe someone abducted her. What we haven't established, yet, is a timeline of events. If you can help, we'd be grateful."

"I see." Rosie frowned. "She didn't come to the riding school after she left Church Stretton."

"Did she want to?"

Rosie snorted. "Oh, I daresay she did." She folded her arms.

"Why do you say it like that?"

"We had words on her last visit. I gave her a few home truths."

"What were the words about, Rosie?"

"It wasn't the riding she was interested in."

"What do you mean?" Yvonne wanted to hear it from her.

"Well, it was a way of keeping contact with *my* husband on weekends. When she couldn't see him in school."

"She had a crush?"

"*Did* she have a crush?" Rosie sneered, spitting the words. "The word besotted comes to mind. Couldn't keep away. She must have thought I was stupid; that I wouldn't guess what she was after, wandering around all doe-eyed, every time he turned up."

"Was your husband aware?"

"He was. He denied it, but it was bloody obvious."

"Did it make you angry?"

"I didn't do anything to her, if that's what you're asking. I gave her an earful and told her not to darken my door again. Justified, under the circumstances."

"You didn't see her again?"

Rosie shook her head. "Nope." She pursed her lips. "How did she die, anyway?"

Yvonne's answer was slow and deliberate. "Her throat was slit."

∼

They sat on the tiny wooden bridge over the stream at Carding Mill.

Yvonne could feel perspiration on her forehead and wiped it with back of her hand, wishing she'd brought a hat.

Tasha dangled her legs over the side, feet not quite touching the water. "So, why are we back here? It's a long way to come to buy me lunch. Wait, you don't think we'll spot the killer, do you?"

Yvonne pulled a face. "No, silly." She giggled. "Though you said he could be a photographer, didn't you?"

"You're pulling my leg..." Tasha narrowed her eyes.

The DI poked her in the ribs. "Yes, I'm pulling your leg."

"So, why did you ask me here on a Saturday?"

"To buy you lunch and bring you up to speed."

"I knew it." Tasha laughed. "Work. I know you so well."

"Three victims, that we're aware of, Tasha. All killed using different methods. One was shot with a crossbow, another had their throat slit, and the last one was strangled. All, within the space of three years. I get the feeling he's preparing us for worse to come." Yvonne sighed, leaning back on her hands. "Am I reading too much into things? I mean, it can't get much worse, can it?"

"The depraved can sink to surprising depths. He'll continue to escalate until you catch him." Tasha clenched her bottom lip between her teeth, hissing out air. "I'm sorry, Yvonne, that's probably not what you want to hear. He's enjoying taunting you. Well, maybe not you, as such, but the police in general. He's an attention-seeker, your guy. He's not going to stop of his own accord."

"One of our suspects met two of the girls through his work. He's a teacher, but he isn't big on art. He's got no paintings on his walls and nothing about him screams artist. His partner is a little scary, though."

"I don't think your perp is a female, Yvonne. The sheer physical work involved in the killing and processing of the victims, makes that unlikely. Besides, a female serial killer is a rare beast."

"I wasn't implying it was Rosie. Her husband, however..."

Tasha nodded. "Give me what you have on him next week and I'll look it over."

Yvonne checked her watch. "Time to eat." Her knees creaked as she rose. "I brought you here for lunch, you know."

Tasha grinned. "I believe you."

"I had dinner with Wyn earlier in the week."

"You did?" Tasha stifled a frown as they approached the cafe. "How did it go?"

"It was okay. He's good company and funny. The suit wasn't right though."

"He wore a suit?" Tasha raised an eyebrow. "Boy, he's *serious*."

"Nooo." Yvonne shook her head. "He kissed me..."

"No way." Tasha stopped in her tracks. "Did you kiss him back?"

"No. It didn't feel right. I stopped him, but I'm worried that I've spent too much time on my own. Maybe no-one will ever be right for me again."

"It'll happen for you, Yvonne and you'll know if it's right. You can't force something like that." Tasha gave the DI's hand a squeeze. "You work too hard. You can't begin a relationship until you slow down. What you need is a holiday romance." Tasha winked. "I'm available in August."

It was the DI's turn to raise her eyebrows.

Tasha grinned and held a hand up. "I'm joking, Detective Inspector."

13
DESIRE

He observed as she selected two oranges, feeling them for firmness and putting them to her nose to savour their vibrant scent. Perspiration itched his upper lip.

He stepped back whenever she looked up. Not that she'd noticed him. He was several aisles away, ensuring enough distance to be just another face in a crowd. One shopper among many.

Placing the oranges in her trolley, she continued to the next aisle, taking the time to read labels and compare prices. He liked that.

He wondered if she calorie-counted. Her figure suggested she might. Slim, but not skinny. Firm, but not muscular. Just the way he liked a woman.

Her bun, drizzled loose, blonde tendrils around her nape, giving her a gentle air. A soft blouse hugged her torso, but not too tight. Skirt, long enough to cover her knees. Shapely legs ended in small heels. She had style and grace.

His basket filled with unwanted items. He would feign impatience at the till and leave it behind. He was here for her. Only her.

She stopped to speak to someone she knew. A male. Smiling, her face animated.

When they continued talking, he checked his watch and gritted his teeth. They'd been conversing for over a minute. She was no different. No different to all the others. She would be fickle like the others.

His knuckles glowed white around the basket handles. Muttering under his breath, he began imagining her destruction.

∼

As Yvonne crossed the supermarket carpark, and opened her boot, she sensed eyes on her back. She swung around, her heart racing. She saw other shoppers going about their business, pushing trolleys or placing bags in the boots of their cars. Nothing out of the ordinary.

She chided herself for being silly and fired up her engine.

∼

The lunchtime bar had quietened down. People had eaten and imbibed their fill, many of them heading back to work.

Terry Mason was aware of her presence, having glanced at her several times during the previous twenty minutes.

He finally approached her, wiping his hands on his trousers and smoothing the sweat from his brow with a sleeve.

"Do you want anything?" He placed his pad and pen on the table.

She noticed a tremor in his hands. "Why didn't you tell me that it was you, who accompanied Nicole Benoit to the Long Mynd on the day she disappeared?"

He sat next to her, flicking a glance to his left and right. "I didn't harm Nicole." He rubbed his lips. "I would *never* have hurt her."

"Then why keep that from us?"

"I didn't want you assuming I had anything to do with her disappearance." He sighed. "Not just you, there are my friends and my employer. The newspapers would have dragged my name and my family through the mud."

"What about *beforehand*? Before you knew someone had hurt her? Why didn't you speak to police when she first disappeared? You must have been aware that people were looking for her? You had vital information."

"I didn't. I don't."

"You'd spent hours with her on the very day she vanished."

He stared at the table. "Do you think I haven't gone over it all, again and again, in my head?"

"What happened that day, Terry? Tell me. Start from when you met her that morning."

He placed his head in his hands. "I had it all planned. My fancy picnic and all the trimmings. Bottle of champagne, picnic blanket, the works. I'd bought a necklace and a ring. The boxes burned a hole in my pocket, I was so desperate to give them to her." He looked Yvonne in the eye. "I wanted to propose. I loved her so much. I loved her from that first night. At the gig."

"Did you propose? Did she turn you down? Is that what happened?"

He shook his head, his eyes unfocussed. "We ate the food. She told me she loved it and that no-one had ever gone to that much trouble for her, before. I took out the box containing the necklace and gave it to her."

"What was her reaction?" Yvonne tilted her head.

"She said it was beautiful, but..."

"But?"

"I noticed confusion in her eyes and lost my confidence."

"Did you give her the ring?"

"No. I left it in my pocket. I decided that I would take her up to the top of Long Mynd, to Boiling Well. I felt, if we walked up there, the setting and the world at our feet... I hoped it would give me the confidence to offer the ring. And, up there with those stunning views, she'd be more likely to accept."

"What happened then?"

"I got on my bike and headed towards the upper carpark. I checked, and she was following. I tethered my bike and set off up the path, on foot."

"What if she hadn't followed you? What then?"

"I'd have gone back to get her." He shrugged. "I wanted it to be an amazing surprise."

"Where was she, when you observed her last?"

"She was on her bike, following along the road beside the stream, a few hundred yards down from the carpark. I was already heading up the hill, on my way to Boiling Well."

"Her killer buried her near Boiling Well."

"I know. I read it in the paper. They buried her in the place where I had waited for over an hour."

"What did you suspect had happened to her?"

"I assumed she had given up on the chase and gone home."

"Did you look for her?"

"On the way down, I kept my eyes peeled. But, I didn't see her."

"She tethered her bike near the car park." Yvonne's eyes narrowed. "Are you telling me you didn't see it?"

He shook his head. "I read about the bike in the papers,

a few days later. I knew something was wrong. She wasn't answering my calls. I dropped by her place a few times and they hadn't seen her. I thought she might have gone home to France, until her family made an appeal for her, on the news."

"You still didn't come forward."

"I thought they'd arrest me and I had nothing useful to tell the police."

"Did she call out to you?"

"I don't think so. If she did, I didn't hear her. I mean, she did when I rode off from the picnic. But, not after that."

"Did she scream? Cry out?"

"What, when I left?"

"Anytime?"

"No."

"What about others? Did you notice anyone else?"

"I did, and I didn't."

"Meaning?"

"Meaning, there were others around. Families and such. But, I wasn't paying them attention. I couldn't describe any of them to you. I couldn't even have done that in the car park. Passersby could have been trees or bushes. My thoughts were all on Nicole and wanting her to marry me."

"Forensics are checking for fibres on the remains that were founds. Will any link back to you?"

"No. At least, if they do, it would only be because we ate together."

"Did you kiss?"

"No."

"The necklace you gave to her-"

"Did you find it?" His eyes widened.

She shook her head. "We didn't recover the necklace,

but I'd like a full description and the till receipt, if you still have it?"

"I didn't steal it, if that's what you think?" His words were forceful, his forehead furrowed.

"I didn't say you did. However, your necklace could help to convict her killer."

"So, you believe me when I say I didn't kill her?"

"We're keeping an open mind, Mr Mason. I may ask you in for a formal interview. On record." Yvonne put her pen down.

"Will you arrest me?"

"It's possible. As I say, you didn't disclose being the last person to see her and, if we match fibres to you…"

"When did you realise it was me?"

"That was with her that day?" Yvonne placed her pocketbook in her bag. "I didn't."

~

DEWI WAS WAITING for her at the station. "How did it go with Terry Mason? Was your hunch correct?"

She nodded. "He *was* with Nicole on the day she disappeared."

"Are we bringing him in?"

"We will be speaking to him again, Dewi, but I don't really think he's a killer, or a stalker or a psychopath. And I believe him when he says that he loved her. However, I don't get the reason he didn't talk to police at the time and, the fact he was with her the day she disappeared, makes him a top person of interest. Get on to the lab. Ask about fibre evidence. I'll speak to Tozer and see if we can carry out a reconstruction at the Long Mynd. Mason said there were families present. Perhaps, we can stir their memories.

"Right you are, ma'am."

∼

SHE CLOSED the door and kicked her shoes off in the hallway. Keys and bag dumped on the table, she stretched and yawned before removing her coat and placing it on a peg.

Weariness pervaded every nerve and fibre and the small of her back was a pure ball of ache. It felt good to be home alone.

Switching on the local news, she crossed the lounge to her kitchen. A cold glass of oak chardonnay beckoned. It might help clear he head, still clogged with the twists and turns of the case. She needed this time to unwind. She needed time.

The soft down-lighting in her bathroom was both welcoming and comforting. Steam rose from the bath as the hot water gurgled in. Another sip of chardonnay and she tugged at the band holding her ponytail, allowing her hair to free-fall around her shoulders and relieve the tightness at the back of her head. She'd had that tightness all day.

She let her blouse and skirt fall in a crumpled heap to the floor and crossed over to the sink, to brush her teeth in her underwear.

A minute later, she was humming the soft strains of a blues song she'd heard on the radio and taking in a lungful of the pine and eucalyptus scent, emanating from the foaming water. She closed her eyes to savour it.

∼

HE HAD to adjust the focus on his Tamron lens. The automatic motor couldn't quite handle the competition between the woman and the crisscrossed wood of the window frames.

He'd enjoyed watching her slip out of her clothing, in a world of her own, swaying to the tune in her head. He wished he could hear as well as see her.

His heart beat faster, his fingers forming circular patches of damp on the camera body. He licked his lips, pushing away the hair from his temples and tucking it behind his ears.

'Click.'

She swayed with her eyes closed, head falling back towards her shoulders.

'Click.' He imagined being in there with her. Taking a hold of her. Crushing that pretty mouth with his own; kneading the bones beneath her pale skin as he pulled her tightly into him.

He cursed under his breath at the steam which intermittently faded his view as he followed the lines of her slim curves with his lens.

She bent to agitate the water, and he had to adjust himself, relieving the pressure in his trousers. A groan came from deep within his throat.

∽

YVONNE TURNED off the taps and grabbed two thick towels from the shelf, placing them within easy reach of the bath. She dragged her hand through the foamy water, checking the temperature, before crossing to the window and closing the blind.

14

FIBRES

Callum handed her a fresh report from the lab. "Just in, ma'am. Looks like they found something on the clothing of Nicole Benoit."

Yvonne flicked open the folder and spread the contents on her desk, her eyes at once drawn to the close-up photographs. They showed the smooth-edged, magnified hair. She muttered under her breath, "Thank you, God."

They had confirmed the hair as being human, but it was not the victim's. Accompanying the brief report was a DNA trace.

"Thanks for this, Callum. Has someone run the trace through the offender database, yet?"

"It has, ma'am, and nothing came up." Callum placed his hands in his pockets. "But, at least we now have *something* we can compare to suspects."

"This is superb news. Can you ask the lab to rule out all SOCO personnel, just as a precaution and, also, we'll need hair and a DNA sample from the chap who discovered the body. Let's make sure it's not his."

"Will do, ma'am."

"Anything back for the other victims, yet?"

"Not yet, but it won't be long now. They were typing up the report on Sharon Sutton's remains, when I telephoned them yesterday and they mentioned possible fibre evidence."

"This gets better." Yvonne pursed her lips. "Let's keep the momentum going."

~

Yvonne drummed her fingers on the desk, clicking her tongue and sighing, as she waited for someone to answer the phone. This was one time when she hoped Hanson wouldn't be too busy.

"Roger Hanson." He sounded gruffer than usual.

"Hi, Roger. It's Yvonne. I hear they've found foreign fibres on the clothes of Sharon Sutton?"

"Sharon Sutton..." There was the sound of shuffling papers. "That's correct. They isolated two black trouser fibres. However, they weren't on her clothing. They were wedged in the hole drilled through the pelvis, trapped between the wire used to attach the femur to the pelvis, and the edges of the hole."

"So, what are we saying? Do we think the perp's trousers were up-close and personal to the pelvic bone?"

"Pretty much. Like, maybe he was... dancing with the bones?"

"Dancing with the bones?" Yvonne frowned. "We do get the weird ones, don't we?"

"You can say that again. I've run a trace on the fibres and we think we've narrowed down the manufacturer and rough date of purchase. That's the good news."

"What's the bad news?"

"Several, country-wide, off-the-rack, high street stores were selling them at the time."

"Oh."

"Hm. Still, it's another piece of the puzzle. We'll just keep working on it. If they purchased the trousers new, it would have been around two years ago."

"What about Katie?"

"We're working on her now. We'll get back to you as soon as."

"I'd appreciate it. Thanks, Roger."

Yvonne put the phone down and sat back in her chair, hands clasped behind her head. She suspected that the crimes were about ownership of the victim. An ownership that didn't cease with the victim's death.

15

A MOTHER'S LOVE

Susan Denham stood in the reception area of Newtown station, eyes puffy. A screwed-up ball of tissue protruded from the sleeve of her sweatshirt.

"I'd like to see DI Giles, please."

The civilian behind the desk grimaced. "I'm sorry, that won't be possible. She's about to go-"

"It's all right, Steven." Yvonne appeared in the doorway, coat and bag, tucked under her arm. "I haven't gone, yet."

She walked over to Mrs Denham, taking in the sunken eyes and tear-stained face. "How can I help?"

Susan took out the tissue and scraped it under her nose. "You might think I'm crazy, but…" She paused, eyes flickering, as though she was fighting for the right words, "I'd like to… I'd like to see my daughter's reconstruction. Would that be possible? I'd like to touch her. I never got the chance to say goodbye to her. Seeing her face would… It would make all the difference to me." She clasped her hands in front of her, searching Yvonne's face.

The DI could see how earnest Susan was, and her heart

went out to her. The request made perfect sense. "I don't have access, Mrs Denham."

"Susan."

"Susan. We don't have it here in the station. It's with the anthropologist who made it."

Mrs Denham's mouth turned down at the corners. She appeared much older than her years and more lined than the last time Yvonne had spoken to her. She looked about to cry.

"I tell you what. I'll call him and find out if we can go over there sometime today."

"Thank you." Susan sighed with relief, her shoulders relaxing.

"Wait here. I'll be right back." Yvonne gave her a reassuring smile and returned to the office upstairs.

"That was quick." Dewi raised his eyebrows.

"I haven't been out, Dewi. There's something to attend to first. I need to make a quick phone call."

Dewi frowned. "Why not use your mobile?"

She pulled a face. "Forgot to charge it and the battery is almost dead. I'll charge it when I get back."

Wyn wasn't answering his work phone. She hung up and dialled his mobile.

It took several rings. "Wyn Sealander."

"Hi, Wyn. It's Yvonne."

His voice softened. "Well, hello. I was just thinking about you and wondering if you would get in touch. Is this business or pleasure?"

"Business, I'm afraid."

"I feared as much." He exaggerated a sigh.

"Wyn, Susan Denham has come into the station. She'd like to see your reconstruction of her daughter for herself, today. I was wondering if we could pop down as soon as possible?"

"But..." He cleared his throat. When he continued, his voice sounded more cold. Distant. "Not today. She can't see it today."

"I could show her-"

"I lock the studio and I'm in Swansea. The key is in my pocket. I'm sorry..."

"Maybe tomorrow?" The DI fidgeted through the extended silence that ensued.

"I tell you what, why don't I call you tomorrow and tell you when it will be convenient?"

"Okay, tomorrow, then. Good. Thank you." She hung up, a frown darkening her features.

Dewi came over. "Is something wrong?"

"Not really." She sighed. "Susan Denham came all the way here for nothing. She's got to come again tomorrow."

∾

BACK IN RECEPTION, Susan was crestfallen.

"I'm so sorry." Yvonne placed a hand on her arm. "We can't get into the workshop. The anthropologist isn't there, today."

Steven, on reception, whistled to get her attention.

She walked over to him. "What is it?"

"Do you want the spare?"

"Spare key? To the workshop? Have you got one?"

"Yes." He walked over to a metal cabinet and opened it, searching along the rows until he found what he was looking for. "There you go." He held out the keyring.

"Stephen, I could kiss you." She grinned. "I didn't even know we had one."

He smiled and winked. "We have spares to all of our premises."

"Thank you." Her smile lit her face. "Come on, Susan. Let's go."

~

The room smelled of old wood, chemicals, paint, clay and Wyn. Yvonne filled her lungs.

SHE LED Susan down the aisle between the benches and stopped at the tiny form, covered in a white dust sheet. "Are you okay?"

Susan nodded.

"You can remove the sheet whenever you feel ready." Yvonne stepped back, allowing the other woman some room and a little privacy.

Susan took a deep breath. The cloth shook as she lifted the edges, her movements slow and reverent.

Yvonne held her breath.

"My God." Susan's hands flew to her face, as she stepped back, open-mouthed.

The DI watched on tenterhooks.

"This could almost be her. She's..." Mrs Denham reached with trembling hands, stopping just inches from the clay form. "Can I... Can I touch her?"

Yvonne walked forward until she was at Susan's shoulder. "Please, go ahead."

Hands still shaking, Katie's mother felt her daughter's likeness with her finger tips as a blind person might, exploring the forehead, the eyelids and down each side of the face. Her thumbs traced along the lips, her fingers cupping the chin. She bent to place a gentle kiss on the forehead, tears wending their way, once more, down her face. Saliva strings stretched between her lips as her mouth formed an anguished hollow. No sound emanated from the cavern of pain.

Susan stayed with the model for several minutes before wiping her face and returning to Yvonne. "He's done an amazing job, your anthropologist. Even the eyes are hers. Thank you."

Yvonne touched her shoulders. "You're welcome, Susan."

"Promise me you'll find who hurt her. Promise me you'll find the person who murdered my daughter."

Although they'd always warned her against doing so, Yvonne whispered, "I promise."

～

WYN CALLED her at nine-thirty the following morning.

"Hi, how did it go in Swansea?" she asked.

"Did you take Mrs Denham to the workshop?"

"I did. Turns out, the station has a spare key. I took that. Hope that was okay?"

"How did she react?"

"It blew away her."

"Yeah?"

"She thinks you did an stunning job."

She heard him exhale. "Well, that's good."

"Your work gave her a second chance to say goodbye. A chance, the killer had taken away. I was proud of you."

"You were?"

"I was."

"Well, that's good. Yes, that's good."

His lukewarm response wasn't what she expected.

Maybe his trip to Swansea had made him tired. "If you like, we could go for a drink. Perhaps, one night this week?"

He cleared his throat. "I *would* like that. I'd like that a lot."

"Is everything all right? You seem on edge."

Wyn grimaced. "My department at Dundee University called me, asking when I'm going up there. They're finishing a paper and models for a museum and need my input."

"Oh." Yvonne pursed her lips. "When do you go?"

"They'd like me next week."

"What about the case?"

He shrugged. "Will you want me over the next few weeks?"

"Well, I..."

"You could always call them and say you need me here longer. It might be better coming from you." He tilted his head.

Yvonne frowned. "Really? Are you scared of them?"

He sighed. "They're very persuasive."

"Do you have their number?"

"Wait there, I'll get it for you."

16

DUNDEE UNIVERSITY

Yvonne dialled the number for Dundee University. It took several rings for someone to answer the phone. She shifted her weight several times, tapping the heels of her shoes on the floor.

"Professor Robson's office," a female answered.

"Ah, professor, I..."

"Hang on, I'll put you through."

Yvonne pursed her lips.

"Professor Robson."

"Hello, professor. My name is Yvonne Giles. I'm a detective inspector with Dyfed-Powys police."

"Hello."

She cleared her throat. "I understand that Wyn Sealander is one of your post-doctoral employees?"

"Er, yes. That's right."

"He's helping us with an investigation. His work has been excellent."

The professor grunted. "Has he helped you solve your case?"

"No, but the victims have a name, thanks to Wyn. We couldn't have identified them without him."

"He's a true professional. Dedicated to his work. He takes his time and he's one of the best reconstruction artists in the country. Most of us use CGI these days, but not Wyn. He still prefers the feel of clay. I'm glad he's been able to help."

"He has. We were hoping to keep him for a little while longer? If that's okay with you?"

Another grunt. "We're working on an historical figure for a national museum. I was hoping he'd be available to help us. Will he be finished with you soon?"

"Perhaps in a few weeks. Would that work for you?"

The professor grunted again. "You're still working a murder case?"

"Serial murder case."

"I see. I guess, we can wait a while longer. Please ask him to get in touch though. We need to chalk a few dates in the calendar. I don't like open deadlines."

As she hung up, Yvonne wondered why everything had to be so complicated.

17

SUSPECT DNA

Dewi placed a steaming mug down on the desk next to her. "What's with the frowny face?"

Yvonne surfaced from her reverie. "Dewi-"

"I brought you some tea. You look like you need it."

"I was miles away, wasn't I?" The frown lines dissipated.

"Want to elaborate?"

"Something, Mrs Denham said."

"Go on..." Dewi pulled up a chair.

Yvonne grimaced. "I don't know."

Dewi laughed. "Now, you're losing it."

"I know I'm not making much sense. What I mean is, something's been niggling at me, since I spoke with her. The trouble is, I can't remember what it was and I can't remember when she said it. I've checked my notes from the first interview and there's nothing in them that rings a bell. The last time I saw her, I didn't take notes."

Dewi rubbed his chin. "Why don't you call her and ask?"

"I will, Dewi, but maybe not today. She's been on an emotional rollercoaster these last few days and she needs a little space. I'll call her in a day or two. It couldn't have been that important, but I remember feeling curious."

"Well, drink up," Dewi ordered. "We've got a date with Tozer's team. They've completed DNA tests on Nicole Benoit's friends and the results are in."

"Already?"

Dewi pulled a face. "Don't get your hopes up, just in case."

∼

TOZER LED them into the main office. In contrast to their own, it was large and populated by at least twice as many officers.

"I've emailed across a copy of the results. Would you like to help interview him?"

"You have a suspect?" Yvonne leaned on the edge of his desk, her arms folded.

"The hair we found on Nicole's clothing, matches Terry Mason. He's now top of our list."

"Well, that's great." Dewi patted Tozer on the back. "Can we see the report?"

"Sure." Tozer reached for a thin file from his desk. "The identification is pretty conclusive."

"He admits being with her that day." Yvonne accepted the file. "They had a picnic together. The hair could have transferred from his blanket."

"Agreed." Tozer nodded. "However, we didn't find a single trace of anyone else. Not one. He is the only person with a *proven* connection to her on the day she disappeared. He's got to be suspect number one."

"Is he here?" Yvonne handed the file to Dewi.

Tozer grabbed a pen and pad. "Yep, he's in interview room one."

"Okay, let's hear what he has to say."

～

Dewi took up a viewing post in the room next door while Tozer and Yvonne interviewed Terry.

"You told officers you hadn't seen Nicole's bicycle, tethered in the upper car park at Carding Mill."

"I didn't see it." Terry shook his head. He fumbled with a plastic cup of water, spilling its contents on the tabletop.

Tozer leaned back in his chair. "Yet, you had tethered your own bike there."

"I know."

"Would you have recognised Nicole's bike, if you had seen it?"

Terry nodded.

"Describe it to us."

Terry screwed his face up in concentration. "Well, if I remember rightly, it was a purple bike with a basket on the front. White- or silver-coloured... The basket, I mean."

Tozer nodded. "That's right. Her bike *was* purple. So, you had waited for over an hour at Boiling Well, then walked back to the upper car park and you didn't see her or her bike?"

"No."

"Yet, you untethered your bike and rode it out of there. Didn't you think it odd that you didn't pass her on the way home from Carding Mill?"

"Yes. I thought it strange at the time. My head was full of all sorts of stuff. I wasn't thinking straight."

"No, you weren't."

"I know what it sounds like..." Terry hung his head.

"What does it sound like?" Tozer asked.

"You think I'm lying because I didn't check for her bike on the way back."

"Why didn't you check, Terry?" Yvonne asked, her voice soft.

"I didn't check because, in my mind, I'd messed up and confused us both. I assumed she'd left, fed up of my antics up the Long Mynd. I assumed she'd gone home. I thought I'd messed up my chances of asking her to marry me. Under the circumstances, I'd kind of expected her to go."

"You said there were several families around." Yvonne checked his statement. "At what point did you try to contact her again?"

"I sent the first text as soon as I got home."

"And she didn't reply."

"Right. I didn't hear from her. The last time I had any contact was when I saw locking up her bike, at the upper car park."

Tozer tutted. "Why didn't you stop and allow her to catch up?"

"I told you, I wanted to surprise her. Wanted her to wonder what was going on. Then, I could pop the question at Boiling Well. I was younger and a lot more foolish than I am now. I thought, if she followed me, the setting and the question would blow her mind." He looked up at the DI. "I loved her. I did. Please trust me. I did not harm her. I would never harm a single hair on her head. She was everything. My entire world."

"Explain how your hair found its way onto her clothing." Tozer leaned forward, hands together, lips resting on his fingertips.

"It must have been on my picnic blanket, or maybe one blew onto her from me, whilst we were eating."

"Did you have physical contact that day?"

Terry shook his head, the corners of his mouth turned down. "No. So many times, I have wished that we had. I wished that I had taken her into my arms, told her I loved her and kissed her. I still wish that with all my heart. Maybe she'd have cut me off. Maybe, I'd have escorted her home, and she'd be my wife, now. Maybe, she'd be someone else's wife. But, at least she'd be alive."

"DS Tozer, may I have a word?" Yvonne asked.

Tozer nodded. "Interview suspended at twelve-fifteen."

∽

"I THINK he's being honest with us." Yvonne levelled her gaze at the DS.

"I agree." Tozer sighed and ran his hand though his hair. "Which is disappointing. We'll let him go without charge, at least for the moment. However, he remains high on the suspect list."

Yvonne nodded. "I understand. But, if he is the killer, he's one hell of a convincing liar."

"Agreed."

∽

"YOU LOOK AMAZING." Wyn smiled, his gaze intense, as they met after work for the promised drink.

"Thank you." Yvonne coloured, glad she had chosen a dress this time. Sea-blue, it complimented her hair and eyes.

"Where would you like to go?"

She shook her head, embarrassed that she hadn't even thought about it.

"I was thinking maybe Lakeside? We can eat and walk there." He flicked his head towards the office. "It's well away from here."

"We can't drive if we're drinking-"

Wyn nodded. "We could book a taxi. If we take your car home, we can book a taxi from your place?"

"What about your car?"

"We'll get the taxi to drop you back home and then me back home. I'll get the bus into Newtown in the morning. I'm sure it won't kill anyone, if I'm late in, for one morning. Does that sound like a plan?"

"It sounds very sensible." She smiled at him, pleased to be doing something different for an evening, with someone who was growing on her.

Situated along a lane, off the Newtown to Welshpool road, The Lakeside bustled. They chose a table near the windows where they could hear themselves speak.

Wyn took her coat, placing it over the back of the chair.

The DI gazed through the glass facade. The setting sun cast a gorgeous, amber reflection on the water of the lake. She eased her feet out of stilettos, relaxing in her seat as the waiter took their drinks order.

"I think we made a good choice." Wyn unbuttoned his shirt sleeves, rolling them up to his elbows.

She nodded, closing her eyes and exhaling. "This is what I need, Wyn. A quiet meal with a friend."

"How's the case progressing? Got a long list of suspects?" He took a sip of his beer and grabbed two copies of the menu, handing one to Yvonne.

"We've matched fibres to an ex-admirer and close friend of Nicole Benoit. Trouble is, I don't believe he killed her.

They haven't finished testing but, to be honest, I'm not that hopeful. I think none of the people we've looked at are capable of murder."

"Anyone can commit murder, Yvonne." His eyes were on her face. "Under the right circumstances."

Yvonne pursed her lips. "Or, the wrong circumstances. We're not talking about a crime of passion, or even murder motivated out of greed or envy. These murders represent more than that." She turned her gaze to the window. "Our killer takes pleasure in terrorising whole neighbourhoods. He's shown, even after several years, he still considers those victims his property, to use or display as he sees fit. It's ego, control, and a love of the macabre. I mean, there's dismemberment, and then there's," She frowned. "what *he* does. It's as if he enjoys the processing as much as the murder itself. Perhaps, more so. He must spend days at it. Cleaning and threading. Our killer has a love of the gruesome."

"Any connection between his victims?" Wyn took another sip of his drink.

"No. Well, only that they *were* his victims, were female, and they came from within a fifty-mile radius of each other." She sighed.

"I'm having the steak." Wyn grinned.

Yvonne sat upright. "Oh god, Wyn. I'm so sorry." She blushed. "Here I am, banging on about work. We should eat, drink, and enjoy a night off."

"It's no problem. What do you fancy?"

She perused the menu, struggling to choose. She plumped for Plaice Veronique, a fillet of plaice, grilled with butter and flour; served with a white wine and grape-cream veloute.

"You haven't touched your wine." Wyn accused, shaking his head.

"Are you trying to get me drunk, Wyn Sealander?" She tutted, smiling as she took a sip of her oaken-chardonnay.

The food was excellent and Yvonne understood why the restaurant, on a golf course, had such a good reputation.

After they finished, Wyn asked for the bill.

"I'll pay half. I *always* pay my way." Yvonne picked her bag up from off the floor.

"This is on me." Wyn stated, his face set. "You can pay next time."

"Next time?" Yvonne laughed. "What makes you think there'll be a next time?" she teased.

"Won't there?" He appeared crestfallen.

"We'll see."

"Come on." He took her hand. "Let's go walk by the lake."

The water had taken on the reddish-purple hue of the sky, as the sun had all but disappeared from view. There was a lot more cloud cover, compared to that when they arrived.

They dawdled by the lake, taking in the smell of grass, mown that day. Yvonne leaned into him and he took her hand.

"Penny for your thoughts?" he asked, swinging her hand backwards and forwards.

She gave him a wistful smile. "I was just thinking it's so nice to get away. Even, if only for a few hours."

"You spend a lot of time alone?" he asked, turning around to once more walk beside her.

"More time than is healthy for me."

"You have friends?"

She nodded. "And family. I should see them more often. When I'm working complex cases, days become weeks and weeks become months. I realise I haven't seen them for so long..." She grimaced. "I spend half my life feeling guilty."

He nodded. "It can happen to the best of us."

"What about you?" she asked, pushing stray hair behind her ears. "Do you have a family?"

"I do. I don't see them enough, either. Look, over there..." He pointed.

Yvonne strained to see but didn't spot what he was pointing at. She had the distinct feeling he had changed the subject. "What did I miss?"

"A large fish broke the surface. May have been a pike."

A crack reverberated around the sky.

"Oops." Wyn looked up, pulling a face.

The rain began in a sudden gush. Large, punishing drops.

Wyn took off his jacket and draped it over her, grabbing her hand, as they dashed back to the restaurant.

He stopped in the doorway, pulling his jacket back to expose her face and hair. "You know," he said, his voice soft, "yours are the most amazing eyes I've ever seen."

Yvonne blushed. "Oh, they're just eyes." She tried to avert her face.

He gripped her chin, moving it back so he could stare down at her. "They are deepest blue and surrounded by a dark ring of browny-green. They are stunning." He placed a kiss on her lips before opening the door so they could get into the warm and dry.

∽

AFTER THE TAXI had dropped her off, the DI ejected her shoes in the hallway. She paused, before entering the lounge, confusion flooding her mind.

She told herself it was just the wine. After several glasses, she felt a little tipsy. At least, she didn't have to worry about work the next day, it being Friday night. She was glad that Wyn had been a gentleman, and that she hadn't had to fend him off.

She remembered what he'd said about her eyes. Were they that striking? She crossed to the hallway mirror and peered into it.

She remembered what Susan Denham had said to her and ran through the lounge to the notepad on her kitchen island and jotted down two notes to herself. Call Tasha, and contact Mrs Denham on Monday morning to ask about her daughter's eyes.

Following this, she took a brief shower and ascended to bed.

~

"Tasha Phillips." She sounded rough.

"Hi Tasha, it's Yvonne. I was wondering how you were?"

Her friend's tone lightened. "Yvonne. Good to hear from you. Well, I'm having a lot of fun here, in my cottage. Not."

"What happened?"

"We had a massive storm and water's coming into the cottage. I've tried stopping it with sandbags, but the storm coincided with high tide and my defences were pathetic. I've got almost a foot of water in here."

"Oh, Tasha. I'll come right away."

"Don't do that." Tasha sighed. "There's little you can do. I'll wait for the water level to drop before doing a cleanup and book into a bed-and-breakfast for a day or two, once I've telephoned my insurance company."

"I coming down right away. Don't argue with me." She hung up the phone.

~

Yvonne parked her car in a lay-by, on the road above Tasha's cottage, and got her wellies and a large flask from the boot. The drive had been interesting, there being a lot of water on the windy roads, between Newtown and Aberdovey.

She picked her way down to the cottage, through mud, water, and debris, and knocked on the door. The water was half-way up her boots and it was difficult to tell if it was receding or still rising.

Tasha came to the door, muddy streaks on her face and sleeves rolled up to her elbows.

"Oh, Tasha." Yvonne threw her arms around her friend and Tasha burst into tears.

Yvonne continued to hold her as she sobbed, waiting for the shaking to calm down before pulling back to look into the psychologist's face.

She had never witnessed Tasha crying before. It surprised her, tugging at her heartstrings. The psychologist appeared lost as though she wasn't sure what to do next.

Yvonne felt her hands. "You're cold... Right, come on, I've got homemade chicken soup in this flask. It'll warm you through."

Tasha sniffed. "It's not that cold, but I've had no power and no way of cooking or boiling a kettle, the last couple of days. The cold has crept into my bones."

Yvonne poured soup into the cup from the top of the flask, keen to get warmth into Tasha as soon as possible.

"That smells good." Tasha blew across the top before drinking.

The DI peered into the cottage behind. Tasha had put a lot of her possessions on high surfaces, but the water had ruined much of her furniture. It smelled of a mixture of sea and sewage.

She swallowed hard. "I'm so sorry this happened to you, After all the hard work you put into this place, it's devastating."

Tasha rolled her sleeves down. "I couldn't believe it, watching all that water coming in. I know it'll get sorted, but it's time and hassle and some of my furniture is beyond saving."

"Finish your soup and grab what you need to bring with you. You won't need much, you can use whatever you need of mine. You're coming home with me. We can deal with your insurance company and coordinate your cleanup from my place."

"You'd do all this for me?" Tasha replaced the cup on top of the flask.

"Without hesitation. You're always there for me and I won't let you face this crisis on your own. You're in no fit state to drive, so I'm taking you in my car and I'll bring you back whenever you need me to, okay?"

Tasha hugged her. "I can't thank you enough. You're a wonderful friend."

18

THE EYES HAVE IT

"Can I come in?"

Susan Denham stepped back into her hallway, allowing Yvonne to go inside.

"Thank you for agreeing to see me again at such short notice." Yvonne followed her through into her tiny kitchen.

"I wasn't expecting another visit, so soon." Susan crossed the kitchen, to fill her kettle and switch it on. "Cuppa?"

"That would be nice." Yvonne nodded.

"Who killed my daughter?" Susan asked, her back to the detective.

Yvonne shook her head. "We don't know yet, Susan. I wish we did. I came here to ask you something."

Susan poured water on the tea bags. "Do you have sugar?"

"Just milk, thank you."

Yvonne waited until Susan Denham returned to the kitchen table with the tea.

"What did you want to ask me?" she placed the mugs on coasters and took a seat.

"When you examined the reconstruction of your daughter, you stated it was an amazing likeness."

"I did..." Susan's eyes narrowed, her head tilting to one side as though trying to work out where this was leading.

"You appeared struck by the eyes, in particular."

Susan nodded. "They were amazing. Your guy had really captured my daughter's eyes."

"Tell me about them."

"Sorry?"

"Her eyes. If you were to describe them what would you say?"

"Katie had vivid blue eyes. Blue irises with a grey ring around them. Her eyes would change with the weather. Sometimes blue, sometimes more grey, but always vivid. Why do you ask?"

Yvonne pursed her lips. "I was wondering if that was why the killer chose her... for her striking eyes."

Susan shrugged. "I don't know."

The DI stayed while Susan showed her photographs of Katie, puffing up at the ones with school trophies.

Yvonne struggled to engage because of the ideas tumbling like washing in her head.

As soon as she was able, she said goodbye, and drove as fast as was legal back to the station.

∽

"Dewi, can you get Nicole Benoit's family on the telephone? Ask them about her eyes and what colour they were."

"Ma'am?" Dewi raised his brows.

"I want specifics, Dewi, as accurate a description as possible. If they can send us a photo, even better. Ask them if they were mixed colours and if there were any imperfections. Oh, and I need the information as soon as possible."

"What are you up to?"

"I'll tell you when I'm sure of myself."

~

Dewi found her staring out of the office window, her brow furrowed in thought.

He pulled out his notebook. "Okay, you ready?"

The DI swung round. "Go for it."

"Well, according to Yvette Benoit, Nicole's mum, Nicole had bright-amber eyes with tiny black flecks in them. She said there was no other colour, but in bright sunlight, they appeared yellow. They stood out."

"Thank you, Dewi." Yvonne returned to the window.

"Ma'am? Is something wrong?"

"Give me a minute. I'll come and find you."

"Right."

~

Yvonne ran her hands through her hair, chewing her lip, going over conversations and seeing the faces of Nicole Benoit and Katie Denham in her mind.

She grabbed her car keys and took the stairs two at a time, picking up the spare key to the workshop from Steven, before heading out.

~

She gave the door two raps and waited.

No answer.

Just in case he hadn't heard her, she knocked again, louder this time.

Still no answer.

She twisted the key in the lock.

The familiar smell of wood, paint and clay greeted her. She chided herself for feeling like she was breaking and entering.

With trembling hands, she lifted the sheets that lay over each of the reconstructions, standing back to take them in.

There they were. Nicole, with bright amber eyes. She peered more closely. Tiny black flecks. She drew a sharp breath.

Then, to Katie, whose blue-grey eyes appeared just as her mother had described.

A knot formed in her stomach as with hands, even more shaky than before, she replaced the covers on the models and retraced her steps to the door.

As she headed to the car park, her head wrestled with the mashed-up thoughts fighting within. Things making sense. Things not making sense.

Wyn's address was on the outskirts of Llanfair Caereinion. She took out a piece of scrap paper from her pocket and typed the postcode into her satnav. Finally, pocketing the note, she fired up the engine and set off. All the while, her heart banged in her chest.

19

CONFRONTATION

The more she thought about it, the more plausible it became. And yet, she didn't want to believe it. As she parked her car close to Wyn's country cottage, she called it in. There were risks and ridiculous risks. He may be innocent, but if he wasn't?

She telephoned Dewi at the station.

"What? What are you doing out at Llanfair? And, why am *I* not with you?"

She could see Wyn's car from where she was parked. He was home. "Dewi, I'm outside Wyn Sealander's home address. I'm in my car. I'll wait for you to come. This may be something or nothing, but I would appreciate your presence, when I talk to Wyn."

"What are you up to?" Dewi's voice deepened. "This sounds ominous."

"You know how impressed everyone was by the accuracy Wyn's reconstructions? Well, I wonder if they were *too* accurate. He had painted their eyes in exact detail, even before we knew who the girls were. It may be nothing, but I want to speak to him about it."

"Is that why you asked me to talk to the Benoit family?"

"Yes."

"Don't go there on your own. I'll be there as soon as I can. Give me half an hour. Don't go in there."

Yvonne nibbled her fingernails as she watched for any signs of movement at the house. She pressed the window down just a little, listening for any sound.

The front of the cottage looked sedate, even pretty. White-painted sash windows, flowers in the borders of a well-trimmed lawn. Red-painted front door. A stream gurgled nearby.

Feeling foolish, she planned how she might duck down below the dash if the door opened, or she saw movement at the window.

She remembered their walk by the lake. The way he bent to kiss her. His comment about her eyes.

'Tap. Tap. Tap.'

She jumped in her seat, heart banging against her rib cage. Wyn Sealander was peering through her side window and smiling at her.

She stared back. Frozen. Not sure of what to do next.

He narrowed his eyes and tilted his head to the side. "Yvonne?"

If she didn't get out, she would give herself away. He might make a run for it or, worse, might try to attack her.

She took a deep breath and opened the car door. "Wyn."

"DI Giles. Well, I wasn't expecting this. I mean, I missed you and I hoped you missed me, but..." He moved closer. "Hello, again." His boyish grin had her doubting herself.

"I was passing by," she said, her voice husky. She cleared her throat. "I thought perhaps you'd put the kettle on?"

He grinned, his eyes flicking over her face. "A cup of tea, it is."

He led her into a medium-sized sitting room, with a low ceiling.

A putrid smell, like rotting meat, hit the back of the throat. The odour of death. She suppressed her gagging reflex, putting the back of her hand to her mouth and turning her face away.

He caught her looking toward the flower-patterned, sofa. "Rented place. What can I say? The furniture came with the cottage." He shrugged, his eyes studying her profile.

"It's cosy." She forced a smile and perched herself on the edge of the sofa, pulling her skirt over her knees.

"I don't get disturbed here," he said, before leaving the room.

She swallowed hard. A faint ticking emanated from somewhere in the room. She looked for the clock. Dewi ought to be there within twenty minutes. She fumbled for her mobile phone and pressed the redial.

"There's no signal I'm afraid." Wyn was back, hands in his pockets. "Waiting for the kettle to boil." He explained. "You could use my landline, but it's not connected."

"It's okay, I was just checking the time."

"Eleven."

"Thanks."

A whistling came from the kitchen. "Oops, that's me." He left the room.

Yvonne opened her bag. Cuffs and mace. She placed her hand around the mace and took several breaths to steady her hands and heart.

"Here, you go." Wyn placed a tray on the coffee table in the centre of the room. "Sugar?"

"Er, no, thank you."

"Are you sure you're all right? You seem tense." He swirled the teapot before pouring into two mugs.

"Do I? I'm just tired. Thank you for the tea," she said, accepting her mug.

He took a sip of his. "Mm, that's good." He smiled at her. "Hope you like it. It's Assam."

"I'm sure I will." She watched her hand shaking, as she brought the mug to her lips, hoping he hadn't noticed. She blew across the top of the mug before taking a sip. In her mind she pleaded with Dewi to get there.

"This is such a lovely surprise. I'd been thinking about you. I wanted to show you this." He rose from his seat and reached past her, as though looking for something from the sideboard.

She pulled the mace out of her purse too late. He held a noxious cloth to her nose and mouth, pushing her back in her seat, with his forearm to her throat. Her mace sprayed the air. She flailed at him and passed out.

∽

Dewi pulled up behind Yvonne's car and got out to look for her.

The DI was not in her vehicle. He tried the door and found it unlocked. Her keys were still in the ignition. She'd taken her bag.

He ran to the door, banging it with a fist, placing his ear against it to listen. Nothing, save his own blood thudding in his ears.

He ran round the back of the cottage. Wyn's car was not there.

He kicked at the door. "Yvonne? Yvonne?" He shouted down the lane. No respond.

He pulled out his mobile and called the station. "Callum, I need armed back up. Now."

"Where are you?"

"I'm at Freesia Cottage, just off of Mount Road, outside Llanfair Caereinion."

"What's the postcode?"

"I don't know the bloody postcode." Dewi ran a hand through his hair. "It's Wyn Sealander's address. If Llanfair station is open today, ask an officer to come over, straight away. I'm on my own until the cavalry arrive. Yvonne is missing. Something about Sealander concerned her. She was going to wait for me in her car. Her car is empty and the keys are still in the ignition. And, Callum?"

"Sir?"

"It's just possible she's in Sealander's vehicle, a black Nissan. Get the reg from Steven and get it broadcast to all units. Find out which cell towers have detected their mobile phones. Inform the DCI of what's happening. This is serious. Yvonne's life is in danger."

"Bloody hell... I'm on it."

20

GIRL IN THE HOLE

Yvonne's head throbbed. She blinked several times, to stop the world swimming. A moan escaped her. Shoulders on fire, she realised he'd secured her hands behind her back and she was naked. No, not naked, she was in her underwear.

Pulling her hands was futile and it hurt. She leaned back, turning her head towards the rusty radiator, he'd fastened her to. Beneath her, a polythene sheet crackled when she moved. It covered most of the concrete floor.

The room was lit by strip-lighting. That explained the background hum. Its light hurt her eyes.

Workbenches ran along each side of what appeared to be a garage. To her left stood a tall clamp-and-stand with arms protruding at various angles. An electric drill lay next to it, plugged in.

She closed her eyes, willing her head clear.

Wyn strode into the room, wearing a wax jacket and holding a crossbow.

She thought he would shoot her and strained against the ties.

He took off his jacket and leaned the crossbow against the wall. "When did you realise it was me?"

"What was you?"

"Come on, Yvonne. You're not a child. That's the reason you're here, isn't it? I knew, the moment I tapped on your car window. The question is, what happens now?"

"Where am I?"

"This is my *other* workshop. We're in the woods. Miles from anyone, in case you're wondering."

"More officers are on their way... Armed response." Her eyes shone in defiance.

"If your colleagues storm this building, another girl dies." He stared at her, his eyes unblinking.

"What do you mean?" She levered herself onto her knees, wincing as the cable ties chaffed her wrist.

"This." He took out his mobile phone, tapping and flicking, until he found what he was looking for. He held it in front of her face.

Yvonne's breath caught in her throat. A young woman peered up from a hole in the ground, up to her thighs in water and smeared with mud. Although the footage was silent, the contorted face made it obvious the girl was in pain.

"Who is that? What have you done to her?"

"She's insurance." His eyes were black.

Yvonne groaned. "Let her go, Wyn. Let her go, please. You've got me."

He shook his head.

She bowed hers. "They won't storm this building while I'm in here. They'll negotiate with you. Let the girl go."

He turned away.

"She'll die of hypothermia. Who would that benefit?

Haven't you destroyed enough lives?" She pulled hard against the plastic ties. They bit into her wrists.

"Your friends may find us, but they won't find her. If they kill me, she's a goner. You and your colleagues would have to live with that."

He picked up the crossbow and put it under her chin, raising her eyes to meet his. "We could have been great together."

"Is that with me alive or dead?" Mucous dribbled from her nose. It itched her upper lip. She tried wiping it on her shoulder, but couldn't quite reach. The crossbow chamber was empty, a small comfort.

He wiped her lip with his thumb. "There's work to do." He pointed to the clamp. "That is where I'll process your bones."

"There won't be time for that." She spat.

"You think?" He moved his face close to hers. "I took the sim card out of your mobile phone before I left the cottage." He turned back to his workbench, taking hold of a cloth and a bottle.

"No. Wyn, you don't need to drug me again," Yvonne stuttered, wide-eyed.

"Wyn, please..."

∼

WHEN YVONNE DIDN'T ARRIVE at Bank Cottage Tea Rooms, where they'd agreed to have lunch, Tasha tried her mobile.

No answer.

This wasn't like her friend. The psychologist's gut told her something was off.

She called the station, just in case the Yvonne had forgotten lunch and become embroiled in work.

Callum answered. "CID."

"Hi, sorry to bother you. It's Tasha. I was expecting Yvonne to meet me for lunch. She hasn't arrived. Is she there?"

Callum's voice cracked. "We're concerned about her, Tasha. She went up to Wyn Sealander's place and we haven't heard from her, since. She told Dewi she had concerns. Now, she's missing and so is Sealander's car. Dewi had agreed to meet her up there. He's still up there."

A tight knot welled in Tasha's stomach, legs threatening to give way. "Oh, my god. Callum, let me help."

"I'm sorry, Tasha, I don't see what you can do. We're running a trace on her mobile and armed response units are en route to the Llanfair area. The DCI has gone up there."

"I could talk to Llewellyn. Can I have the address?"

"I'm not sure I can give you the address," Callum paused. "You could go to Llanfair police station. Dewi is meeting armed units there. The DCI will also be at the station until they decide where they need to go. If go now, you may get to them before they move elsewhere. If not, I'll check with Dewi and find out where they're heading. I'll ask whether I can let you know where they are. Ring me if they're not in Llanfair."

Tasha put the phone down in a daze, wondering why Yvonne hadn't talked to her about her suspicions. It wasn't like her, to not canvas the psychologist's opinion. Tasha ran to her car and set off to Llanfair.

DCI LLEWELLYN'S SHOULDERS HUNCHED, as he paced up and down, shouting orders into his mobile phone. His hair jutted at various angles as he ran his hand through it, sighing.

Tasha waited for him to take a break. "Chris?"

He turned round, dark patches under his eyes. "Dr. Phillips..." He flicked his head back in surprise. "What are *you* doing here?"

"I'm sorry, I found out Yvonne was missing and came to see if I could help."

"I see." He flicked his eyes from side-to-side, thinking.

"I'd like to mediate. I'm fully trained."

"Tasha, we don't even know where they are. Her phone hasn't pinged a tower for over an hour. We think he either destroyed the phone or took the sim card out. His, too."

"They can't have gotten far, can they?"

"It looks like he took her in his car. We've got armed officers combing the area around the cottage and we're carrying out door-to-door enquiries in and around the Llanfair area. The problem is, they could be anywhere. We've sent out a countrywide alert. That hasn't yielded anything, yet."

"Have you searched the house?"

"It's being searched, as we speak. I've just spoken to Dai. They've found nothing out of the ordinary, except a nasty smell."

"Can I wait with you?"

If he heard her, the DCI didn't show it. He had his phone to his ear once more. "Callum, find out who Wyn banks with. Ask payroll for his account details. Speak to the bank and get a hold of statements, covering the last few months. It's just possible he's rented a room, a garage or a lockup somewhere. If so, the regular payments will show in his statements. Trace anything that looks relevant. Thanks."

He turned back to the psychologist. "He has to process

the bodies somewhere. I'll bet that's where he's taken Yvonne."

Tasha swallowed hard.

∽

AMANDA SELBY SCREAMED. Racked with pain, her contorted body and shivered. She had lost the feeling in her lower limbs and fell into the muddy water, now two feet deep. Each time she dropped, she hoisted herself up again, refusing to die in that hellhole.

Rain tumbled from the sky in heavy, thunderous droplets. Clay-rich soil prevented the water from draining. The level continued to rise. She sobbed, calling out to somebody. Anybody. Her hoarse cry didn't carry far.

Not knowing where she was, she fought the sleepiness overtaking her. Listening to the stream nearby, she raised her feet, one at a time, to keep warm. Dark thoughts pervaded her head. She might not make it.

21

FATHERS

He sat with his side to her, working at the bench. She lifted her head, fighting to focus drug-addled eyes. He didn't appear to notice her coming round.

Movements slow and deliberate, he filed and polished drill bits, blowing dust from the ends, before placing them on the bench next to him.

It surprised her to hear him humming. She listened for the tune, hoping to make conversation. Her thoughts were on the desperate girl in the ditch. She had to save her.

"That looks painstaking," she began. "I admire your patience."

He didn't turn though he paused filing. "My father was an engineer." He blew on a drill bit.

"*Was* an engineer? What does he do now?" Though difficult, she kept her voice as steady as she could.

"Now?" He pushed back from the bench, not looking in her direction. "He grows grass and flowers."

She frowned. "Retired, then?"

"My father's dead." He turned to face her. "Gave up,

when I was ten. My mother drove him to an early grave. You won't understand what that's like. He was everything." He twisted back to his drill bits.

"I could surprise you." She shifted on the floor, easing the ache in her right thigh. "My father killed himself, too. I was a teenager."

"Oh, I see. I get it." Wyn snorted. "You're about to tell me you know what I've been through. You'll try to get into my head. I hate liars. Telling me your father killed himself is low."

"I'm not lying. It doesn't matter if you don't believe me. It's true. My dad killed himself after my mother had an affair."

His chair shot round. "Stop with the crap. I've had it with women who try to manipulate me." He spat saliva, his mouth twisted in anger.

She looked for the right words. "Wait, I tell you what, why don't go into my bag. Get my purse. See for yourself."

He stared at her for several seconds before leaving the room. He returned a minute later with her bag.

"What am I looking for?" he asked, his eyes unblinking.

"Open the zip. There's a folded newspaper cutting. Please be careful, it's old and fragile." She held her breath.

After reading it, he clicked his tongue against his teeth. "So, you were telling the truth..."

She nodded. "It took me a long time to forgive my mother. I needed the anger because to let go of it was like letting go of my father. But I was only hurting my family and myself. My dad's death had not been my mother's intention. She'd fallen out of love with him and into love with someone else. My dad couldn't accept it and, for a long time, neither could I. It's not that it doesn't hurt anymore, just that I see it differently... and feel better for it."

"Well, good for you. We can't all be so magnanimous."

"Tell me about your father."

He snorted.

"I gave you my story, please give me yours. If you intend killing me, you can at least do that?"

He turned his eyes from her. "I was ten years old. My mother had taken to drink. She would swear and curse and smash stuff. I'd hide under the bed. My father took it all, the abuse, the drinking, and bringing back other men to the house. He took it until he could take it no longer." A tear escaped down his cheek.

"I'm sorry..." She meant it. She meant it for the little boy that Wyn had been. The little boy who'd hidden under the bed.

Wyn let out a groan from deep within. An anguished, animal sound. "*I* found him. He'd slit his wrists, along the veins. There was so much blood. It was everywhere, all over the walls, the floor, the furniture. He'd cut through to the bone. I saw white beneath the severed flesh."

He continued, "He was still alive, when I found him. I didn't know what to do. I grabbed towels and wrapped them around his arms. I watched those towels fill with creeping, red blood." He took a deep breath, exhaling through his teeth. "I ran to a neighbour and banged on their door until they answered. By the time we got to back to him, his lights had gone out forever. His eyes just stared at the ceiling."

"Wyn, I..."

"I ran and ran. I kept running. I stayed out all night. When I got home, my mother was there with her sister. I ran into the kitchen and took the largest knife I could find from the drawer. If they hadn't stopped me, I'd have taken her life, right there. Instead, social services took me into a secure children's home. It was a prison. Every night, I dreamed about my father, and his lifeblood ebbing from him. Every night, I tried to save him all over again."

Yvonne's cheeks and chin were wet with tears and mucous. "Is that why you kill women, Wyn? Are you killing your mother? Are you taking revenge for your father's suicide?"

He strode over to her and slapped her hard to the side of her head. "Don't psychoanalyse me."

She cried out, pain coursing through her temple, her ears ringing. "The girl out there, the one you put in a hole, is not your mother. She's an innocent who hasn't had the chance to make a family of her own. That girl has harmed no-one."

He sneered. "She won't get the chance to hurt anyone, now, will she?"

"She might lead a fulfilled life with a good husband and well-adjusted children. But, you're playing god. What are you? A saviour of men? What? You think your crimes justified? What about the women hurt or killed by their partners? Do you think their daughters should become killers of men? Let me tell you, there's a far higher percentage of female victims."

He raised his hand, and she turned her face away, expecting a blow to come.

Instead, he backed away from her, returning with a cloth to dry her face.

∼

"Dance with me." He threw the cloth to the floor, kneeling to slide an arm around her waist.

She looked into his eyes. "If I dance with you, will you release the girl?"

He matched her gaze with his own, his pupils so large, his eyes were black.

"I will release you from the radiator." His voice was low, threatening. "If you fight me, the girl dies."

He crossed to a bench, returning with scissors.

He released her left wrist. For one moment, Yvonne contemplated punching him and running for her life. What stopped her was the girl. She might live, but the girl would die. She was calm as he freed her right arm from the radiator.

At last, she could stand, relieving the ache in her thighs and lower back. Her shoulders throbbed, her hands having been so long behind her back.

"What's your favourite music?" he asked, sliding an arm around her; pulling her against him.

She didn't know. At that precise moment, she couldn't recall any. That part of her brain wouldn't work. She shook her head.

"Ever watched, 'The English Patient'?"

Her expression was blank.

"It's a film by Anthony Minghella."

She narrowed her eyes.

He was humming again. Placing a hand at the back of her head, and one around her waist, he whirled her round the room, polythene crackling beneath their feet. It was awkward. She tripped on his feet.

He tightened his grip, raising her until her toes barely touched the floor. He kept her going round, both arms encircling her waist, her head horizontal with the floor. She felt light-headed. Powerless.

He slowed, to place a kiss on her throat. "It's almost time, my love."

He let her go.

She fell to the floor. "You said you would release the girl."

He narrowed his eyes. "Her name is Amanda."

"Please, release Amanda."

He pursed his lips, staring at her. "I'll put you back on the radiator. Try anything and she dies."

Yvonne held her breath as he took out fresh cable ties, fastening her once more to the cold metal.

He pulled on his coat and grabbed the crossbow. "I'll release her, but it'll mean your mates pouring all over this place. You and I will die all the sooner."

She nodded. "I know. I still want you to release her."

He turned to leave.

"Please... take her a blanket?"

He grabbed an old, paint-spattered sheet, before leaving the room.

∼

"Did you do it? Is Amanda free?"

"She is." He pulled out his mobile phone, placing it in front of her face. "Want to watch?"

She didn't know whether she wanted to watch, afraid of what she might see. The stiff muscles in his face had her fearing he had killed the woman. A sob came from inside her.

He pressed play on the video.

The footage bobbed up and down in time with his footfall as he'd approached the hole in waterlogged ground. Then came the cries for help, sounding like the yelps and screams of a wounded animal.

The footage switched to ground level as he had placed the phone down to lower a rope into the hole. Yvonne heard the gruff instructions he shouted to Amanda, to tie the rope around her waist.

Amanda resisted, at first. Perhaps, afraid of his next move.

Yvonne held her breath, The woman appeared thin and dirty, her eyes, sunken. She hunched over as though expecting violence. Even through the camera lens, the DI could see how she wobbled, frightened to take a step.

Wyn took the blanket from under his arm and draped it over her. There was no tenderness in his movement. It was a cold thing holding no meaning.

He put the phone away. "See? I kept my word. Now, get ready to keep yours."

He clicked the phone off.

"What... What happened to her after that?" She looked up at him wide-eyed, pulling against the ties holding her to the radiator.

"I told her to keep walking, until she found someone."

"Did you give her food? Water?"

"No."

She turned her face to the floor. "What if she's injured?"

"She's free. That's what you wanted, isn't it? That's what you got."

He lifted her chin. "What about your side of the bargain?"

Yvonne whimpered. She couldn't bear the thought of his touching her.

He knelt to release her from the radiator. "Move, and I *will* hurt you."

She fought to keep her body still, knowing she mustn't appear weak, even though she had nothing left with which to bargain.

He lifted her to her feet. Free from the radiator, but with her hands strapped behind her back, she stared in defiance.

"Where were we? Oh yes, we were dancing." His eyes bored into her. He gripped her with force and they danced an awkward waltz.

She followed his lead, her movements disjointed. Eyes tight shut, holding back tears, she prayed her team were close.

He pulled her to him and put his face in her neck.

22

YOU WIN, YOU LOSE

Outside, armed police were closing in, running between the trees at the edge of the wood. They were in a quiet dell, not that far from the lane where they had parked their vehicles.

Dewi and the others halted in the long grass. They could just see the lockup through the trees at the wood's edge.

He groaned in frustration. "This is taking so long."

The DCI pulled a face. "I feel your pain, Dewi, but if we hadn't traced the owner of the lockup, we'd still be searching for her."

Tasha nodded, her face, drawn. "We can't rush this. He has nothing left to lose. Go in like the cavalry and he'll kill her. He has weapons. We can't take that risk."

"Agreed." Chris Llewellyn looked about them. "Let's let the ARV guys do their job. This is what they're good at."

"Wait, look!" Dai pointed to where a figure had emerged from the trees.

Tasha drew in a sharp breath. "Is that Yvonne?" She was about to call to her, when the DCI put a hand on her arm, shaking his head.

"It's not Yvonne."

The figure stumbled, disappearing into the long grass. An armed officer rushed to help her and get her to safety.

DCI Llewellyn strode to meet them.

Armed response moved into position, their weapons primed. Clad in black, they communicated with hand signals.

Tasha, the DCI and Dewi stayed a few hundred metres back, watching from the long grass.

A dog team also waited by the road. Obedient animals, standing with their handlers, ready for action.

A chopper whirred overhead. It created swirling circles in the grass before moving off. A myriad blue lights peppered the road behind.

∼

"What's your name?" DCI Llewellyn escorted the girl to a waiting ambulance.

"Amanda Selby," she whispered, shivering under the old sheet.

"Amanda, were you in that building over there?" He pointed towards the lockup.

She shook her head. "I was in the... ground. I was in a grave." Her face contorted as she cried.

Two paramedics dropped a stretcher on the ground and released the spring to turn it into a trolley. They wrapped a foil blanket around Amanda and hoisted her up.

As they asked her questions about her condition, the DCI headed back to his team, shaking his head.

"Did she have information about Yvonne?" Tasha asked, hands at the sides of her face.

"Nothing. She told us her name is Amanda Selby, and someone had put her in a grave. Once she's medically assessed, we'll find out more."

THE RESPONSE TEAM leader spoke to the DCI over the radio, informing him they were in position and that the only window was the small one next to the lockup door.

"Can you blow a hole through the back wall?" Llewellyn asked.

"Not without risking hurting your DI," came the answer.

"Roger that." DCI LLewellyn took a deep breath and strode back to the others. "They're ready. They have a sniper watching the window and the door."

"I'll take the phone to the lockup." Dai straightened his jacket.

"No." The DCI was emphatic. "I'll ask the response team. They're the ones with the armour."

Tasha admired Llewellyn. The shine on his brow and upper lip was the only sign of the stress he was under. Her own forehead was just as damp. Sweat soaked the hair at Dewi's temples too, as he paced about.

She looked back at the lockup. There was no sign of movement. The thought passed through her mind. What if they're already dead? She shuddered. "Not Yvonne," she whispered to herself. "God, not Yvonne."

∼

AN ARMOUR-CLAD OFFICER tossed a phone to the foot of the lockup door.

DCI Llewellyn shouted through a megaphone. "This is the police. Are you all right in there? I want you to know if you need anything, we'll do our best to get it for you." He listened for any sound before continuing. "We have placed a phone outside the door, so you can talk to us. Tell us what you want. I will turn this off, now. Get the phone when you are ready to talk."

23

LIFE OR DEATH

"Did you hear?" He snorted. "Your *friends* have arrived. They're waiting for me to get the phone, so they can blow my head apart."

She cleared her throat, "I'll go." It was practically a whisper. She changed position, trying to ease the discomfort in her bladder. It was hours since she'd been to the toilet.

"What if your trigger-happy colleagues blow *your* head off?"

She grimaced. "They won't do that. They want to talk."

He crawled over to a cabinet under his workbench. He turned the key in the lock and pulled out two crossbow bolts.

Pulling back the mechanism, he chambered one bolt, and crawled back to Yvonne. He put the crossbow on the floor behind him before releasing her from the radiator.

He bound her hands behind her back, with thick twine, allowing her enough length to have limited forward reach. She was glad of the change though felt as though her shoulders might no longer function.

The edge of the crossbow dug into her neck. "That thing

got a safety catch?" she asked, as he escorted her to the door. The acrid, urine-stink of sour sweat made her want to vomit.

His voice was a whisper in her ear. "We don't need safety. We won't make it out of here."

She stood, shuddering, at the door.

"This bolt will destroy your neck," he stated, "unless you do as I tell you."

She nodded, clenching and unclenching her fists to increase blood flow and reduce the strain in her arm muscles. A deep breath helped calm her, and she closed her eyes.

"Walk over and pull back the lock. Do it nice and slow."

She did as he said, fighting with the stiff mechanism, one hand at a time.

It opened with a clank and she fell back.

"Wait," he ordered, listening again. "Open it enough to get the phone. If you run, I will kill you before you get three paces."

She saw figures in the distance as the light poured in. She did not communicate with them. Ducking back inside with the mobile phone, she handed it to Sealander. Through her mind, ran thoughts of how she might tackle him, now she had more movement in her arms.

As though reading her thoughts, he levelled the crossbow at her. "I wouldn't, if I were you."

The phone rang in his hand. He put it to his ear. His eyes stayed on her face. "Yes?" he growled into the handset.

The crossbow still pointing, he put the phone to her ear. "They want to hear from you. They're worried I may have hurt you. Speak to them."

"Hello? Hello, it's Yvonne."

"Yvonne, thank god. I-" the DCI began.

He yanked the mobile from her. "That's enough."

He put the phone back to his ear. "She's alive, but she won't be if you try anything." He turned to Yvonne, "They want to know if we need food or water?"

She nodded. "I'm so thirsty."

He spoke into the phone. "No, we don't need food or water. What do *I* want? I want time with your detective inspector."

He clicked the phone off and pulled her towards him. "Where were we?"

"Wyn, don't be crazy. They will blow a hole in the wall and pile in here. They will kill you."

He shook his head. "No, they won't. They won't risk your life." He pushed his head towards her as though to kiss her.

She pushed him hard with both hands. It was enough to move him back.

He pointed the crossbow, arm locked. "I will kill you now and then I will kill myself."

"Wyn," she pleaded, her eyes earnest, "you witnessed things, horrendous things, that you should never have witnessed as a ten-year-old boy. But, you could give yourself another chance." Tears streamed down her face. "You could give that little boy another chance."

"Right. Another chance to spend my life in prison. And I *would* spend my life in prison. I am a danger to women. I'll *always* be a danger to women."

"You wouldn't be a danger to women in prison."

"What kind of life is that? Confined, nothing to do."

"You could continue to learn. Hell, you could even continue to model the faces of the dead. Those with no name... Make amends."

He laughed, his face screwed up. "Listen to yourself. They wouldn't let me model faces. Think of the headlines. That would go down well. Not."

"So, that's it. You'll give up?"

His eyes searched her face. "There's something about you. You got under my skin."

She swallowed hard. "Stay with us. Stay in the land of the living."

The phone rang again.

He held it in front of him, glaring at it.

"Would you like me to take it?" she asked, "I could speak to them. Tell them you will surrender yourself."

He put the phone to his ear. "What?"

He looked at the DI. "Someone called Tasha?"

"Tasha." Her eyes lit up. "Let me speak to her? Please?"

He put the phone to her ear.

"Tasha?"

"Yvonne. Are you all right? Has he hurt you? Are you injured?"

"I'm fine. In need of the toilet. Otherwise, okay."

"We've got the door and the window covered-"

"I'm making progress-"

He snatched the phone from her and switched it off. "Making *progress*?" He tilted his head. "You make it sound like an experiment."

"I'm trying to save your life, Wyn. I'm thinking of your ten-year-old self."

He narrowed his eyes. "Careful, I might think you care for me."

She turned her head away. "I do."

∼

THE GRASS WAS flat around Tasha's feet. She paced up and down, working through conversations that might end the siege.

Dewi threw his hands in the air. "He can't keep this up much longer, he's got to be tiring."

"Don't bank on it." The psychologist shook her head. "He could keep this up for days. I'm surprised he didn't ask for food or drink, though."

"It's frustrating, not knowing what is happening in there." Dewi took out a handkerchief and wiped his brow.

The DCI rubbed his chin. "Tell me about it. We've got to get him to switch the phone back on."

Tasha shook her head. "It's a waiting game. He'll switch the phone on, again. Guaranteed. He'll be wondering what we're doing and the effect his actions are having on us. Give it time."

"What if he kills her?" Dewi frowned.

"I'm sure he won't." Tasha shook her head. "If he wanted to kill her, he'd have done so already. He's accepted he will die. He's just buying time with Yvonne. I think he's in love with her."

"I wonder what she's thinking?" Llewellyn crossed his arms.

"She's terrified but, if I know Yvonne, she'll be working on him. If I'm right, and he is in love with her, she'll have as good a chance as any at getting him to give up."

∽

"I NEED THE TOILET." Yvonne shrugged. "I'm sorry, I'm desperate."

He scratched his head. "Over there, under that bench. There's a bucket."

She frowned.

"I'll keep my back turned, if that's what's worrying you. You need to go. So, go."

She crawled along the floor to the bench. She feared standing. The snipers might mistake her for Sealander. She retrieved the bucket with difficulty and, checking that Wyn had his back to her, relieved herself.

The experience should have been degrading. Under the circumstances, it wasn't.

She replaced the bucket under the bench.

"Better?" he asked when she returned.

"Yes." She sat on the floor. "What happens now?" she asked.

He appeared deflated, like the fight was leaving him. She couldn't believe the man in front of her had committed the heinous acts he had. That he had destroyed several women and taken an evil pleasure in it.

She pursed her lips. "What changed in your life?"

"What do you mean?" He asked, his face impassive.

"When I saw where you had buried Nicole Benoit and Katie Denham, my first thought was that you had chosen those places so the world would never find them. They looked like *forever* graves," she continued, "but, you dug them up and put the bones on display. It makes no sense."

"It need not make sense to you." He delivered the sentence cold.

"Still, I'd like to understand."

He met her words with silence.

"Something changed, didn't it?" she persisted.

"I told you, don't analyse me."

"I'm sorry." She bowed her head. "Does your mum know the effect her actions had on you as a child? Did she ever apologise? Have you seen her since?"

He swung his head towards her, spitting the words, "She's dead!"

Yvonne closed her mouth, wondering whether she ought to say she was sorry. She decided against it.

"She died six months ago," he added, his voice less harsh. "I'd listen to her dancing in the living room, with whichever man she'd brought home, while my father was in bed, pretending to be asleep."

"Where were you, when she did that?"

"I would sit on the stairs. Thinking of ways to hurt her."

"So, each time you hurt a woman, you were hurting her?"

"Does that make you feel good? Piecing it all together? Nice, neat little answers? Does the world makes sense again? Does that give you closure?"

The blood rose to her head, and she clenched her fists. "The closure isn't for me, Wyn. It's for the mothers and fathers; brothers and sisters; lovers and friends. For all the people who lost a part of themselves when you *took* the lives of the women they loved. *You* did that. *Your* sadistic, perverted, selfish needs destroyed countless lives. It was *you* who desired closure after a dysfunctional childhood. You filled *your* holes with the blood of the innocent."

His mouth hung open. "Why don't you say what you mean? Perhaps, I'd be in less danger out there... You know, we're the same you and I. Both of us lost our fathers and spent our time being angry at our mothers."

"We are nowhere near alike." Her eyes blazed. "I *save* lives. *You take* them."

He bowed his head.

"Give yourself up." She sensed a shift in the dynamic. "Take your punishment. Do your time."

"Where are you going?" he asked, as she rose and headed towards the door.

"I'm leaving," she answered. "I don't care what you do to

me, I'll take my chances. But, if you take my life, you'll continue to dwell in the hell you blame your mother for."

"Wait," he ordered. "They might shoot you by accident. I'll tell them we're coming out."

She watched him pull the phone from his pocket and put it to his ear. "Don't shoot. We're coming out. Your detective inspector will be in front."

24

DISASTER

She drew in her breath, as he grabbed her, once more placing the crossbow to her neck. "You don't need that," she said, through clenched teeth.

"Yes, I do."

He pulled back the bolt on the door, pushing her through it.

She blinked, as the bright sunlight stung her eyes.

He made the weapon obvious to those watching. Holding it at right angles to her head, his forearm around her neck.

Without warning, he stretched out the arm with the crossbow, aiming towards the line of police. He pushed Yvonne to the ground.

"No!" Yvonne yelled, as the first shots rang out. She got up as fast as she was able.

Bullets smashed into her right shoulder and left thigh.

As she fell, the world became a blurred vision of grass, trees, sun and sky and Tasha, running. More bullets whizzed through the air above.

The last sound she heard was Wyn's body crashing to the polythene floor.

25

TIME

Overhead lights rode in and out of focus. Yvonne blinked several times, trying to clear the haze.

A kaleidoscope of shapes, bustling here and there, became nurses in smart uniforms. The daylight fuzz, became the window opposite.

"Hi, welcome back. I thought I'd lost you." Tasha's face leaned in and the DI realised she was holding her hand.

"I saw you running. They could have killed you." Yvonne accused, pushing herself up and wincing in pain.

"Hey... Don't get up. I ran, because I saw you go down and I was desperate to get to you."

"I'm sorry for putting you through that."

"We've got no nails left. You know that. Your team... me... You had us pooing ourselves, big style."

Yvonne grimaced. "The DCI will have my guts for garters."

Tasha laughed. "He'll eat them with a nice chianti." She put a hand to her mouth. "Sorry, that was in bad taste..."

Yvonne chuckled. "It's okay. It's a safe space."

"The doctor said you were very lucky. You clavicle was

smashed, and the bullet that hit your thigh went straight through, without hitting either your femur or your femoral artery."

"Wow."

"Yes, wow. You're one charmed lady."

"And Sealander?"

Tasha shook her head. "I've learned nothing about him, since he was surrounded by officers and paramedics. You were both airlifted here. I don't know if he made it. He took a lot of bullets."

"I heard them." Yvonne pursed her lips. "How long will I be in here? Did they tell you?"

"At least two weeks, I should imagine. But, no, they told me nothing. Even though I bombarded them with questions. They would not let me in to begin with. It's just friends and family. Kim was here, earlier, with the children."

"My sister? Is she coming back?"

"She'll be here soon. They've gone to get something to eat."

"I can't wait to talk to them."

"I'll go while they're here. There are strict limits to the number of visitors. I'm sorry, I implied to the medical staff I was your partner."

"You did what?" Yvonne gave Tasha a stern look which turned into a laugh. "You bugger."

"Kim helped." Tasha grinned.

"She what?"

"Well, they wouldn't let me in."

"I'll have words with the pair of you."

"It helped that I brought a bag with your pyjamas and make up."

"*Did* it now?" Yvonne pulled out her tongue. "Well, since

you're my *partner*, I could do with a sneaky sandwich and a cup of tea. Am I allowed food? I'm starving."

"They've said nothing. I'll check with a nurse and, if it's okay, I'll get you something. Then, will you forgive me?"

Yvonne grinned. "I'll think about it."

∼

"You have more war wounds than many of the army veterans I know." DCI Llewellyn stood by her bed, hands on hips; his tie knot, halfway down his chest. "What did you think you were doing? They could have killed you. I've never known anyone so careless with their own well-being."

"I'm sorry." Yvonne grimaced.

"Meanwhile, *you're* facing months in recovery and *we're* down a brilliant DI, until you're mended."

"I *am* sorry, really, I am."

"On a personal note, Yvonne, I've never been so terrified. I was sure you were a goner. Don't you bloody *dare* do that again?"

"I'll try not to, sir."

"Why *did* you get up, when the shooting started? Are you carrying a torch for Sealander?"

She shook her head. "I hadn't fallen for him, if that's what you mean." She meant it. "I had the urge to mother a tiny boy. A boy who spent long hours sitting on the stairs, watching his life unravel in front of him, powerless to do anything about it. A boy who, at the tender age of ten, witnessed the bloody aftermath of his father's suicide."

"My heart bleeds." The DCI frowned. "Lots of children go through hardship. They don't all turn into psychopaths."

"Yes, he's a monster. But, he was born a blank slate." She shrugged. "I wanted to pick him up and carry him off the stairs, tuck him in with his favourite teddy and a bedtime story. I'm sorry, you must think I'm losing it."

"He's still alive, Yvonne."

"He is?" She stared, wide-eyed.

"I don't get *how*. He's got more holes than a Swiss cheese. He's in intensive care, under armed guard, and appears to be stable. Doctors are sure he will make it. Though, he'll go through months, if not years, of trial, when he's recovered and he'll spend the rest of his life behind bars. However, he's still here because of you. You saved his life."

"I did?"

He nodded. "According to the armed response team, the bullet that hit your shoulder would have turned his lights out... permanently."

"Head shot?"

"Head shot."

∼

"Told you I'd be back." Tasha grinned and plopped a bunch of grapes and two magazines down on the bedside cabinet.

"Good job." Yvonne raised an eyebrow. "The nurses would have suspected that we'd split up."

"Nice to see you're on form." Tasha grinned. "What did Llewellyn say to you?"

Yvonne sighed. "He thinks I'm a hopeless risk-taker. He's pissed at me, right now."

"He'll get over it. He cares about you, you know?"

"How's my team doing?"

"Dewi's acting up."

Yvonne laughed. "Dewi's *always* acting up."

"You know what I mean... He's doing *your* job, while you're in recovery."

"Good to hear everything is in safe hands." Yvonne winced as she changed position.

"Still hurting, then?"

"Just a bit. What about you, Tasha? How are you? Have you sorted your cottage?"

Tasha rubbed her chin. "It's coming along. The cottage is clear and the reparation work has started. I'm still at your place at the moment. I hope that's okay?"

"Sure. Stay as long as you need."

"I'll stay long enough to help you settle back in, when you get home. You will find things difficult, at first."

"Thank you, Tasha." She reached to squeeze her friend's hand. "Thank you for being here."

∼

SIX WEEKS LATER, Yvonne visited the station, on crutches. She wanted to be there, for when the mothers and fathers of the dead girls collected the few bits and pieces that had belonged to their daughters.

"Are you fit enough for this?" DCI Llewellyn asked, a tender look in his eyes.

Yvonne nodded. "I want to do this, sir. I feel like I owe them this much."

"The Benoit family send their thanks and best wishes to you. They can't be here. Nicole's remains are being flown out to France for burial, today."

"And, the others?"

"Susan Denham, and Clive and Debbie Sutton are waiting, through there." He stepped back and allowed her to hobble to where the parents waited in reception.

They stood, as she entered and Susan Denham ran over to her and gave her an awkward hug, afraid of hurting her. "Thank you. Thank you for finding our children's killer."

The DI almost dropped her crutches. She smiled and grimaced, wincing at the pain in her shoulder.

"Oh, God. I'm sorry." Susan stepped back. "I get carried away."

"No need to apologise." Yvonne looked at her crutches. "I can't wait to get rid of these things."

Clive Sutton put pressed Yvonne's arm. "Thank you for finding our daughter's killer. I can't imagine what you, yourself, went through for us... and for our girls. We will always be grateful."

Yvonne shook her head. "You don't have to thank me." She smiled. "Your daughters were amazing women. Their loss broke many hearts. Their deaths affected everyone we interviewed. They miss your girls. I want you to know I don't regret a moment of what happened. I'd do it again in a heartbeat. The killer is where he ought to be and, with your help, we've prevented him from taking the lives of many more. You helped catch him. Without your input, he would have continued taking precious young lives. I am the one who should thank you."

As she watched them leave, the DI closed her eyes, seeing the reconstructed faces of the dead girls. In her imagination, she gave each of them a hug, to say goodbye. Tears welled, but stayed where they were.

"It's good to have closure." Dewi's voice came from behind her.

"Dewi!" She turned, to see him coming over to take his turn in giving her a hug.

His hug was gentle. "You gave us a helluva fright, lady."

She screwed her face up. "Sorry."

"Cup of tea?"

She grinned. "You know me so well."

∽

Keys clanked and scraped.

His back muscles tightened.

The door flew open.

"Here are the papers you requested, Sealander." The prison officer tossed them onto his bed. "And here," he said, handing over the items, "is the needle and thread for your button."

"Thank you." Sealander took the need and cotton. "What about the scissors?"

The officer shook his head. "No scissors."

"But-"

"I'll be back for the needle in twenty minutes, just before lights out. Don't lose it. If you do, you'll find yourself in solitary."

"But-"

The door banged shut, followed by the sound of keys in the lock.

Sealander threaded the needle, biting off just enough cotton for the task ahead. He placed it down onto the small desk in his room and crossed the couple of feet to his bed and the day's newspapers.

She was all across the front pages. The heroine detective making a good recovery. Soon to be back at work

He read the stories out loud, through clenched teeth, then ripped the front pages off.

Two of them carried the same photograph. Taken from the front. She was on crutches, struggling to get somewhere. The others, stolen profile photos. One showed her going into a shop, another, getting into her car. In the last ones, she was entering the station. Going 'for a visit'.

He sneered. Between them all, he had enough for what he intended.

He cursed at the lack of scissors and set to ripping out the images of her, separating the out the bits he wanted.

Then, laying them all out on the tiny desk, he began sewing them together at the edges. Piece by piece. Neat, delicate stitches.

Sweat stood on his brow, the result of the concentration needed to prevent the needle from tearing the tiny strips.

He checked the clock. Two minutes until lights out. The screw would be back any minute.

He placed the gruesome, three-dimensional image of her on his desk, stepping back, when he heard the keys turning in the lock.

"Needle."

He had the urge to stick him with it. Instead, he held it for the officer to take, his shoulders hunched in submission.

The officer studied Sealander as though aware of the dark thoughts churning behind the smile. Cautious, he extracted the items from Sealander's hand.

That was that. The door shut. The lights went out. He made his way to back to the desk, feeling along the surface for the newspaper effigy.

He lifted it up, pressing it to his lips before holding it at arms length in front of him. "This isn't over, Yvonne. It will never be over."

The End

AFTERWORD

Thank you for reading. If you enjoyed this book, I'd be very grateful if you'd post a short review on Amazon. Your support really does make a difference.

Mailing list: You can join my emailing list here : AnnamarieMorgan.com

Facebook page: AnnamarieMorganAuthor

You might also like to read the other books in the series:
Book 1: Death Master:

After months of mental and physical therapy, Yvonne Giles, an Oxford DI, is back at work and that's just how she likes it. So when she's asked to hunt the serial killer responsible for taking apart young women, the DI jumps at the chance but hides the fact she is suffering debilitating flashbacks. She is told to work with Tasha Phillips, an in-her-face, criminal psychologist. The DI is not enamoured with the idea. Tasha has a lot to prove. Yvonne has a lot to get over. A tentative link with a 20 year-old cold case brings them closer to the truth but events then take a horrifyingly personal turn.

Book 2: You Will Die

After apprehending an Oxford Serial Killer, and almost losing her life in the process, DI Yvonne Giles has left England for a quieter life in rural Wales.Her peace is shattered when she is asked to hunt a priest-killing psychopath, who taunts the police with messages inscribed on the corpses.Yvonne requests the help of Dr. Tasha Phillips, a psychologist and friend, to aid in the hunt. But the killer is one step ahead and the ultimatum, he sets them, could leave everyone devastated.

Book 3: Total Wipeout

A whole family is wiped out with a shotgun. At first glance, it's an open-and-shut case. The dad did it, then killed himself. The deaths follow at least two similar family wipeouts – attributed to the financial crash.

So why doesn't that sit right with Detective Inspector Yvonne Giles? And why has a rape occurred in the area, in the weeks preceding each family's demise? Her seniors do not believe there are questions to answer. DI Giles must therefore risk everything, in a high-stakes investigation ofa mysterious masonic ring and players in high finance.

Can she find the answers, before the next innocent family is wiped out?

Book 4: Deep Cut

In a tiny hamlet in North Wales, a female recruit is murdered whilst on Christmas home leave. Detective Inspector Yvonne Giles is asked to cut short her own leave, to investigate. Why was the young soldier killed? And is her death related to several alleged suicides at her army base? DI Giles this it is, and that someone powerful has a dark secret they will do anything to hide.

Book 5: The Pusher

Young men are turning up dead on the banks of the River Severn. Some of them have been missing for days or even weeks. The only thing the police can be sure of, is that the men have drowned. Rumours abound that a mythical serial killer has turned his attention from the Manchester canal to the waterways of Mid-Wales. And now one of CID's own is missing. A brand new recruit with everything to live for. DI Giles must find him before it's too late.

Book 6: Gone

Children are going missing. They are not heard from again until sinister requests for cryptocurrency go viral. The public must pay or the children die. For lead detective Yvonne Giles, the case is complicated enough. And then the unthinkable happens...

Watch out for Book 8 coming in the new year...

ALSO BY ANNA-MARIE MORGAN

More books in the DI Giles Series:

Death Master

You Will Die

Total Wipeout

Deep Cut

The Pusher

Gone

Coming soon : Book 8 in the DI Giles Series